ROSE OF RABY

The first and second books in a saga

about the Yorks, Lancasters and Nevilles,

whose family feud started the "Cousin's War",

now known as the Wars of the Roses,

told by Cecily "Cecylee" Neville (1415-1495),

the Thwarted Queen

Cynthia Sally Haggard

Spun Stories Press
Washington DC 20036

Published by Spun Stories Press

Designed by Cynthia Sally Haggard

Manufactured in the United States of America

ISBN: 0984816909
ISBN-13: 978-0-9848169-0-3

For my dear friend Beth Gessert Franks
for all her endurance of Cecylee

Contents

Acknowledgments

This book took me seven years to write. I could not have done it without the help of many people. The first person who deserves thanks is my friend Beth Franks, a talented writer in her own right, who patiently went through several drafts of *Thwarted Queen*, and made innumerable suggestions for improvement.

Next, I want to thank my wonderful editor Catherine Adams, formerly of the *Iowa Book Doctors* now of *Inkslinger Editing*, for her structural editing of the manuscript early on, and the many helpful suggestions she made then that brought the novel to a new level. This summer, Catherine did a magnificent job in the line-by-line content and copyediting, gently pruning the manuscript to give it what I hope is a polished, professional feel. Any mistakes are my own!

I also wish to thank Lord Barnard of Raby Castle in County Durham for his interest in my novel, and for allowing Clifton Sutcliffe, the docent, to take me on a personal tour of Cecily's childhood home in July 2007. Mr. Sutcliffe showed me the Keep where Cecylee was locked up by her father, and explained to me about the wooden walkways that criss-crossed Castle Raby to make passage from one tower to another easy in the event of a raid. I am also indebted to him for bringing to my attention John Wolstenholme Cobb's *History and Antiquities of Berkhamsted*, in which he quotes *The Orders and Rules of the Princess Cecill*.

I wish to thank the United States Military Academy Department of History for allowing me to use the map of England and France circa 1422, and for Emerson Kent in helping me to find it.

I was privileged to take classes with many wonderful teachers during my long journey with *TQ*. I wish to thank Mark Spencer, professor of English and Dean of the School of Arts and Humanities at the University of Arkansas at Monticello for his class *Successful Self-Publishing*, given during the spring of 2011; Curtis Sittenfeld, author of *American*

Wife, for her sensitive reading of the novel during the *2010 Napa Valley Writer's Workshop*; Amy Rennert of the Amy Rennert Agency for her class *Secrets of Publishing Success* given at Book Passage in Corte Madera CA, during the fall of 2006; Janis Cooke-Newman, author of *Mary: Mrs. A. Lincoln*, for her invaluable help on the end of the novel; Michael Neff, creator of *Web del Sol*, for his wonderful classes on craft at the *2005 Harper's Ferry Workshop*; Junse Kim, who taught *Introduction to Fiction: You Can't Build a House without Foundations* and Otis Haschemeyer, who taught *Introduction to the Novel* at the *Writing Salon* in Bernal Heights San Francisco during the fall of 2004. I could not have written and published my novel without the help of these professionals.

My friend Beth Robertson deserves thanks for sharing her expertise on Chaucer, and her knowledge of subversive activity amongst medieval ladies, who would often read material that would not have pleased their husbands. Such inflammatory scrolls were secreted in the saddle bags of Abbesses and other ladies, who were ostensibly just making a social call.

I wish to thank the following writers for reading the manuscript and making useful suggestions: Kristin Abkemeyer, Myrna Loy Ashby, Sharyn Bowman, Peter Brown, Julie Corwin, Eric Goldman, Joy Jones, Phil Kurata, Nadine Leavitt-Siak, Michelle McGurk, Amanda Miller, Rose Murphy, Nicole Nelson, Dan Newman, Desirée Parker, Walter Simson, Kevin Singer, Judy Wertheimer, Jun Yan.

Last but not least, I wish to thank the talented Heather Hayes for donating her time to model for Cecylee; her friend, Whitney Arostegui, for donating her time to shoot the photos that were used for the cover of the novel; Dave Graham for donating his time to convert my cover images to CMYK mode and teaching me to make the necessary edits; my husband Georges Rey for prodding me to continue with Cecylee, and my sister Melanie, for giving me the idea in the first place.

Plantagenet

Edward III
d. 1377

Edward of Woodstock Prince of Wales "The Black Prince" d. 1376

Lionel of Antwerp Duke of Clarence

John of Gaunt Duke of Lancaster

Edmund of Langley Duke of York

LANCASTER m. **BEAUFORT**

YORK

Richard II

Philippa m. Edmund Mortimer

i) Blanche

iii) Catrine de Roet (Lady Katherine Swynford)

Roger, Earl of March

John, Duke of Somerset d. 1410

Henry Cardinal & Bishop

Joan (see NEVILLE)

Edmund, Duke of Somerset

Edward, Duke of York k.1415

Richard, Earl of Cambridge ex. 1415 m. Anne Mortimer

Anne Mortimer m. Richard, Earl of Cambridge (see YORK)

John, Duke of Somerset

Margaret Beaufort m. Edmund Tudor, Earl of Richmond

Henry, Duke of Somerset

Elizabeth m. John Holland Duke of Exeter

John

Henry, Duke of Exeter m. Nan Plantagenet (see NEVILLE)

Henry VII

Richard, Duke of York m. Cecylee NEVILLE

Henry of Bolingbroke Henry IV

Humphrey Duke of Gloucester

John, Duke of Beford

Henry VIII

Henry V d. 1422

Henry VI m. Marguerite d'Anjou

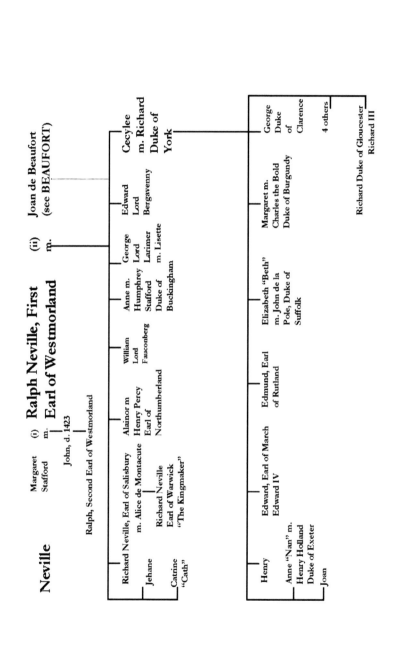

Neville

Margaret Stafford (i) m. **Ralph Neville, First** (ii) m. Joan de Beaufort
Earl of Westmorland (see BEAUFORT)

John, d. 1423

Ralph, Second Earl of Westmorland

Richard Neville, Earl of Salisbury
m. Alice de Montacute

- Jehane
- Catrine "Cath"

Richard Neville
Earl of Warwick
"The Kingmaker"

Alainor m.
Henry Percy
Earl of
Northumberland

William
Lord
Fauconberg

Anne m.
Humphrey
Stafford
Duke of
Buckingham

George
Lord
Larimer
m. Lisette

Edward
Lord
Bergavenny

Cecyle e
m. Richard
Duke of
York

- Henry
- Anne "Nan" m.
  Henry Holland
  Duke of Exeter
- Joan

Edward, Earl of March
Edward IV

Edmund, Earl
of Rutland

Elizabeth "Beth"
m. John de la
Pole, Duke of
Suffolk

Margaret m.
Charles the Bold
Duke of Burgundy

George
Duke
of
Clarence

4 others

Richard Duke of Gloucester
Richard III

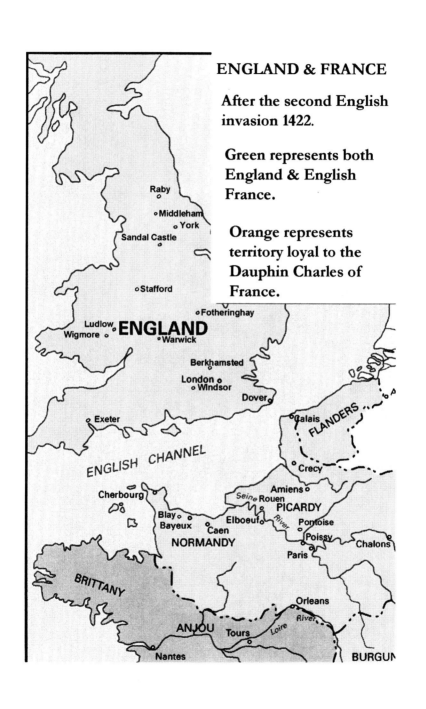

ENGLAND & FRANCE

After the second English invasion 1422.

Green represents both England & English France.

Orange represents territory loyal to the Dauphin Charles of France.

Raby

Middleham
York
Sandal Castle

Stafford

Fotheringhay

Ludlow **ENGLAND**
Wigmore
Warwick

Berkhamsted

London
Windsor

Dover

Exeter

Calais FLANDERS

ENGLISH CHANNEL

Crecy

Cherbourg
Amiens
Seine Rouen
Blay PICARDY
Bayeux Elboeuf
Caen Pontoise
NORMANDY Poissy
Paris Chalons

BRITTANY

Orleans

ANJOU
Tours Loire River

Nantes BURGUN

PROLOGUE
❦ ❦ ❦ ❦ ❦

She useth to arise at seven of the clocke,
and hath readye her chapleyne to saye with her mattins of the daye,
and mattins of our lady;

FROM ORDERS AND RULES OF THE PRINCESS
CECILL
QUOTED BY JOHN WOLSTENHOLME COBB (1883)
HISTORY & ANTIQUITIES OF BERKHAMSTED

Berkhamsted Castle, Hertfordshire
Feast of Saint Joseph
March 19, 1495

Now I am ready to speak, for death will be with me by year's end.

The House of Tudor shall declare this tale a lie. They will say I'm an impostor. Let there be no mistake about my identity. As proof, I lay forth my name in its true construction:

Queen by Right
Duchess of York
Abbess

I am Cecylee—not Cecily or Cicely. My name has been corrupted by those who claim to have the ear of the present King of England, one Harry Tudor, Earl of Richmond, a self-styled King Henry VII. Let those who seek to dismiss my testament compare this sign with the many documents signed as Duchess of York and Queen by Right.

I have had other names. I was born Lady Cecylee de Neville, in May 1415. In the year 1424, I became Duchess of York. Admirers called me the Rose of Raby. Enemies called me Proud Cis. I am the mother of Kings Edward IV and Richard III. I have seen my sons kill their opponents, and even their kin.

Folk think me saintly, for I hear Mass several times a day. I hear religious texts while I dine, I spend hours on my knees in prayer. This causes them to disbelieve some of the unflattering stories whispered about me. Folk are too kind if they imagine that a pious old woman couldn't have sinned. It grieves me greatly to say this, but late in life, while I was living in the countryside as Abbess of a Benedictine Order, I was responsible for the murder of two of my grandsons.

In these pages, I make confession, using my voice and the voices of others important to its weaving.

BOOK I: THE BRIDE PRICE
❦ ❦ ❦ ❦ ❦

"A gracious lady!
What is her name, I thee pray tell me?"
"Dame Cecille, sir."
"Whose daughter was she?"
"Of the Earl of Westmorland, I trowe the youngest,
And yet grace fortuned her to be the highest."

FROM A FIFTEENTH-CENTURY BALLAD,
ANONYMOUS

Chapter 1
Castle Raby, Scottish Marches
The Feast of Saint John
June 24, 1424

Today they tell me I must behave.

I'm not allowed to laugh loudly, stare, or make remarks.

I must put on my best gown, the pink silk damascene with the long train, balance my heavy headdress on my head, and play my psaltery. The king's uncles are coming to visit.

Today, they decide if I'm suitable enough to be made Duchess of York, and maybe queen. Richard Plantagenet, Duke of York, the boy I'm supposed to marry, is only thirteen, but they say he will be the richest peer in the kingdom when he reaches the age of twenty-one.

"But that's not for years," I point out. "I'm only nine years old. Why do I have to do this now?"

"Richard is the king's cousin," Audrey, my mother's maid, tells me. "If the king were to die, Richard would be king. Your father wants to secure your future now."

I sigh. Sitting in stuffy rooms listening to Mama and Papa and all those important people they know wearies me. If you are the Earl of Westmorland, like Papa, and the king has given you the task of guarding the English border against the heathenish Scots, then you must want to know many such people. But I prefer to frolic under one of the huge trees that surround the castle.

I turn my head slightly, and Audrey mutters as she stuffs my thick blond hair into the netting under the headdress. Sliding my eyes to the right, I can just make out the shapes of the trees through the newly glazed windows of our rooms in Bulmer's Tower. Bulmer's Tower is a five-sided tower shaped like an arrowhead that stands apart from the rest of the towers comprising Castle Raby. It can be easily defended from a sudden raid on the castle, so Papa decreed

that all of us should live here. The trees seem small and very
faraway.

Mama enters my chamber, carrying my psaltery. Her
eyes look pink. Silently, she scrutinizes me, her lips pinched,
as Audrey curtsies and steps aside. Then she takes my hand
and leads me up the steep spiral stairs to the solar.

"How much are you willing to pay for her?" says a
deep voice.

Mama clenches my fingers so tightly I yelp.

"That is John Plantagenet, Duke of Bedford, the
senior uncle to the king." Mama, Joan de Beaufort, Countess
of Westmorland, turns me around so that I have to look into
her eyes. "He's just been made regent of France, and rarely
comes to England. It is a high honor for him to visit us,
Cecylee."

"But you don't seem happy," I remark as we peek
through the arras.

Mama shakes her head and puts her finger to her lips.

"Two thousand marks," replies Papa.

Through an opening in the richly woven tapestry, I
find Richard standing in one corner, his hand running
through his hair. For the past six months, he's been living at
Castle Raby. When I asked why, Papa pinched my cheek and
said it would be well if we got acquainted. I try hard to be
pleasant, but he is so serious. He's dressed in black. Couldn't
he think of some other color?

Duke John looks around the solar, his sharp eyes
taking in Papa's glazed windows, the newly installed hooded
fireplace on the north wall, and the rich hangings. He reminds
me of a merchant at a fair.

"Four thousand?" he says.

Papa stares at his lap as if he's just discovered
something fascinating, perhaps a pulled thread, on his silver
and blue robe. Ralph de Neville, Earl of Westmorland, must
never be too quick to compromise.

A cough erupts as a gentleman enters from the door
opposite and bows. I turn to Mama.

"That is Duke John's younger brother, Humphrey Plantagenet, Duke of Gloucester. He lives in England and acts as regent for the king."

"How old is the king?"

"Three years old."

"He's ten years younger than Richard then."

Mama quietly shushes me.

Duke Humphrey smiles at Richard. Perhaps they are friends. I did hear someone say that Richard always stays with him when he visits London.

Duke Humphrey shakes his head.

Richard smiles faintly.

Duke John sighs. "Three thousand?"

"'Tis a goodly sum," says Duke Humphrey. "Three is the sign of the Trinity. 'Tis the perfect number."

Papa strokes his white beard. The corner of his mouth quirks. Then he roars with laughter. "Done. Let us drink to it."

Mama gives me a look, which means to stay here behind the arras and be quiet. She goes to Papa. "You know I am not happy with this."

"Cecylee needs to marry," replies Papa. "This betrothal will make her Duchess of York, and you know where that might lead."

A duchess! I wiggle with excitement. That would make me more important than Mama! She says softly, "I care little for that kind of future. I want my Cecylee happy in her life."

"Don't be ridiculous," snaps Papa.

Duke John looks surprised. He holds his wine cup high in the air and stares at Mama. To my surprise, she kneels.

"She is my youngest daughter, and only nine years old. Do you have to do this now?"

Papa bangs his cup on the arm of his chair, ruby-red liquid sloshing to the floor. "Mind yourself, my lady," he hisses, wagging his finger, as Jenkin rushes to clean it up. "Never contradict your lord in public."

Drawing a handkerchief from her long triangular sleeve, she dabs her eyes.

Papa helps her up, leads her to her seat, and signals for wine.

Mama looks straight at me and nods.

I run into the room. Suddenly all eyes are upon me. I dip a deep curtsey, rising smoothly and without wobbling, the way Mama taught.

Richard bows and smiles, then frowns. I smile back, trying to coax that frown away, and when his features smooth out, I turn to Mama. "What shall I play for the company? Shall I do *I Cannot Help It If I Rarely Sing*?"

Papa slaps his thigh and bellows with laughter.

Mama smiles: "Why not sing *This Lovely Star Of The Sea*?"

Settling onto the window seat beside Richard, I nestle the psaltery in the crook of my elbow, pluck it, and began to sing. I love to sing, it's so good for the spirits.

"This Rose of Raby has spirit as well as beauty," says Duke Humphrey after listening for a few moments.

"She's not shy," replies Papa, smiling.

Duke John winks at Richard. "I know you must be eager to wed."

Richard colors a fiery red, making the gentlemen laugh heartily. I sigh.

"When is the ceremony to take place?" asks Duke Humphrey.

"I wonder if it could be this year," says Papa, "in October, on the Feast of Saint Luke."

I strum my psaltery with a flourish and finish the song.

"What are you going to sing now?" whispers Richard.

"Wait and see." I glance at the adults, who are busy talking, and play softly *I Cannot Help It If I Rarely Sing*.

"Cis!" exclaims Richard, laughing softly. "Your lady mother—"

"It's too late now, isn't it? Shhh. How can I talk to you if I have to sing?"

Richard smiles and sinks back onto the cushions next to me. He looks less serious.

"Where will they live?" asks Duke John.

"Where would you like to live?" whispers Richard.

I think for a minute. I don't want to be far away from Mama. "Do you have a castle close by?"

"I have many castles, Cis. But not here."

"Oh." I turn away. "I don't wish to move."

"I know that you, my lords, have much on your minds," says Papa, bowing. "So I wondered if they could be betrothed rather than married. That way both Richard and Cecylee could continue to live here."

Richard nudges me. "Did you hear what they said?"

I nod and smile. I pluck my psaltery and take a deep breath:

> *A gardyn saw I ful of blosmy bowes*
> *Upon a ryver, in a grene mede,*
> *There as swetnesse evermore inow is,*
> *With floures white, blewe, yelwe, and rede—*

"What is that song, Cis?"

"It was written by Granduncle Chaucer. I made up the tune myself. Shall I teach you?"

Richard puts a hand on my arm, for Duke Humphrey speaks. "Is it not true that you have a large number of soldiers garrisoned here at Castle Raby?"

"Indeed," says Papa, "I am warden of the western march, and I have to patrol the land from here to Scotland."

"I like not the idea of rough soldiers being so close to this pretty rose."

Duke John stares at me. "Why not have little Cecylee and young Richard live at court with their cousin King Henry?"

"But Cecylee will be safe here with me," says Mama, hands tensing on her chair.

"This is a serious issue," says Papa slowly. "It is true that I have a large garrison of soldiers here because of the Scots raids, and because of the lawless nature of this country."

"We would not want our wild rose plucked before her time," says Duke Humphrey. "Young Richard here is close to the throne. It would not be seemly if his wife-to-be were caught in a rough soldier's embrace."

Confused, I turn to Richard. "What are they talking about?"

"Your virtue," he replies, reddening.

"But there is no blemish on my virtue." I frown.

Richard pats my hand. "You would not be able to defend yourself against any man determined to take you. You have not the strength."

"I have a good kick. And I know where to aim."

"Cis!" Richard pulls down the corners of his mouth. He looks strange, but then I see he is trying not to laugh. "How do you know that?"

"Audrey." My mother's maid has been with her for hundreds of years, and knows everything. I ease the psaltery into a comfortable position, strum for a minute of two, and then sing a song I composed to please Mama:

> *I once was in a summery dale,*
> *In one such little hidey-hole,*
> *When I heard a great debate*
> *Between an owl and nightingale.*
> *Their brief was stiff and stark and strong,*
> *Sometimes soft, and sometimes loud,*
> *As either side swelled up against*
> *The other, and cursed each other out.*
> *Letting fly their evil thoughts,*
> *They said the very worst they could,*
> *And on and on about their songs,*
> *They argued vehemently and long.*

'Tis my favorite song, and it always makes Mama laugh. She says it is very old, perhaps one hundred and fifty years old, written by someone unnamed, but I make it my own by strumming loudly on the heavy accents of the poem, particularly the words "stiff and stark and strong". I look up, expecting her grin, but Mama looks pinched around the lips. She signals for me to stop.

"How would you guarantee her safety?" asks Duke John.

"I could give her apartments in the keep for her very own use," says Papa. "They are accessible only through a flight of steep and narrow stairs. There is a guardhouse underneath those rooms, which could be garrisoned by my most trusted men."

Duke John comes closer. "You want this marriage so much, you are prepared to lock your daughter up?"

My mouth opens, I look at Mama.

She stares at the floor, her fingers tensed around the bunched fabric of her silken skirts. Suddenly she looks up and glares.

She glares at Richard.

Chapter 2
Michaelmas
September 29, 1424

I fly upright in bed; something wet has touched my ear. A hound regards me mournfully with his large brown eyes. Laughing out loud, I snuggle up to him in the pile of furs.

An Irish Wolfhound with wiry hair, long legs, and floppy ears, Clavis is a birthday present from Papa. He said, now that I'm growing up, I should have a hound. It would attack whenever I'm in danger, just like in the saying, *they are gentle when stroked, fierce when provoked*. I retorted, who would dare to accost me, the youngest daughter of the greatest lord of the land. Papa said only, better to be safe than sorry.

I lie in my new apartments in the keep, the bed in the main chamber, a large room made of flat white stone. The windows are so high up, I have to angle my head to see the castle courtyards below. I miss looking out at my trees, and I'm tired of the faint stench of latrines that makes its presence felt, even on cold days.

To the right of the window opposite my bed, a door leads to a small room where Jenet sleeps. Next to my bed, another door leads down a steep spiral staircase to the guardroom. When Jenet enters this morning, I hear the scrape of metal and the sound of male voices. She curtseys, pours a jug of angelica water into the bowl, and waits. I turn away, burrow under my furs, and cuddle up to Clavis, who growls appreciatively. I giggle as I count under my breath. How long will it take for Jenet to speak? Once, I counted all the way up to three thousand before my new maid timidly asked if I wouldn't like to wash my hands.

This morning, however, is different. The door bangs as Audrey surges into the room.

"Get up, my lady!" she shouts. "Your sisters, Ladies Catherine and Anne, have arrived!" When she tugs the bedclothes off the bed, Clavis jumps up and barks. I shiver in the damp chill of the large stone room as Audrey calls for hot water to be brought up from the kitchens for a bath.

"My lady's uncle writes beautifully, and in English too, so we can all understand it. Even a humble shepherd can understand what Master Chaucer says, not like those priests forever muttering in Latin." Audrey is small and brown like a sparrow, and never stops talking.

I yawn. "How I long to leave." Audrey attaches the wide triangular sleeves to my gown over the pink silk chemise. "I haven't been allowed out since midsummer."

"You know that's not true, my lady." Audrey ties the laces into a bow. "Duke Richard often takes you out."

I make a face. I want to go out with someone who laughs loud and gallops as swiftly as a greyhound. Richard is always worried about something. He thinks I will fall off my pony if I'm not careful. But I don't want to be careful, I want to soar up into the sky like an osprey. At least today, I'll be allowed out for a few short hours. I wriggle in blissful anticipation, and Audrey mutters under her breath.

"Where is Papa?"

Audrey kneels to adjust the long train of my silver and dark green dress.

"He's ridden out, hasn't he?"

"Never you mind," says Audrey.

"I wish he would ride out more often, so I could visit Mama in Bulmer's Tower."

"Mind your tongue, my lady," says Audrey, motioning for Jenet to drape the fur mantle over my shoulders. "You should not speak ill of your lord father. He rode out at dawn to head off another Percy raid."

"Are they going to attack us?" I ask.

"Mayhap," says Audrey.

"But why?" says Jenet, going pale.

"The Percies and the Nevilles," says Audrey. "They have these huge private armies to stop the heathenish Scots from their border raids. The Percies are supposed to be patrolling the eastern marches and the Nevilles, the western.

That would be all well and good if the Percies and the Nevilles saw eye-to-eye. Naturally, they do not."

"What mean you?" says Jenet faintly.

"They fight each other," I say. "Sometimes they don't notice that the Scots have launched another border raid."

Audrey sits to put her clogs on. "If you've got loads of men roaming the countryside armed to the teeth, you get all kinds of banditry. You get raids, skirmishes, ambushes."

"But in Picardy, it wasn't like that," murmurs Jenet.

"We are not in Picardy, *ma petite*," replies Audrey. "Here, in the far north of England, it is wild, dangerous, unruly. Ungodly, you might call it."

Jenet crosses herself. "If we're going to be attacked, shouldn't we be making ready?"

"Never you mind," replies Audrey. "My lady is in Bulmer's Tower. That can be defended in any raid."

"What about the king?" asks Jenet, drawing close her red woolen mantle. It is her most prized possession, all she had of value when she left Picardy in northern France after the death of her mother to come serve me under the guidance of Audrey, her mother's sister. Audrey tells me that she has around fourteen years.

"The king's writ does not run here," I say.

"And that is why your lord father gave you these fine apartments in the keep, in the middle of the castle, to keep you safe," says Audrey. "Truly, he knows what is best for you." She picks up my train.

"But I hate being mewed up." I pick my way onto one of the wooden walkways that criss-cross Castle Raby. "I want to be free." My voice is taken away by a gust of wind.

"My lady and I speak French, of course," says Audrey to Jenet as they follow. The gusting wind makes the wooden walkway sway. I sway in time to it. These walkways allow the soldiers to patrol our defenses and get from one tower to another easily, but the wind makes the journey somewhat perilous. "But we don't do as some jumped-up persons do, which is to speak loudly in French to show off in front of their servants."

Another gust knocks my cone-shaped headdress to the side of my head. I giggle, for I must look very peculiar. I stop so that Jenet can replace it on my head.

"I would never tell my lady this to her face," continues Audrey as we walk sixty feet above ground, "but do you really want to understand what Master Chaucer says? It's such rubbish! There he is, as bold as brass, criticizing the church. And then there is that vulgar tale told by a miller about the young woman who cuckolds her husband by pretending the flood is upon us."

She pauses to let the material of my train flow down the wooden staircase taking us into the top of Bulmer's Tower.

"Take the Wife of Bath," says Audrey as we enter Bulmer's Tower, "that dreadful woman with her four hundred pounds of linen on her head, her five husbands, and all her talk against chastity. 'Tis proper scandalous, I tell you, and no fit subject for a young lady."

I bite my lips to prevent myself from laughing; if I want to hear gossip, I best look stupid. I take the fur mantle off, give it to Jenet, and enter the solar.

Mama is reading aloud:

> *'You have two choices; which one will you try?*
> *To have me old and ugly till I die,*
> *But still a loyal, true and humble wife*
> *That never will displease you all her life,*
> *Or would you rather I were young and pretty*
> *And chance your arm what happens in a city*
> *Where friends will visit you because of me,*
> *Yes, and in other places too, maybe.*

"It's the Wife of Bath today," mutters Audrey to Jenet.

I curtsey to Mama and sit on the window seat, picking up the tunic left for me to embroider. Truly, it is a glorious day. The sun throws beams of light across the floor where my betrothal gown is laid out in a pool of blue velvet. The betrothal is less than a month away. Yesterday my half-sister Mary, a daughter from Mama's first marriage, finished stem-stitching the hem, which reads *Cecylee, Duchesse of Yorke* in a scrolled pattern. 'Tis very fine.

Audrey takes off her clogs and kneels on the carpet to draw a design for the skirts with her wand of chalk. It looks like a flowery mead with animals. As I am fond of sheep, she sketches in a couple for Jenet to embroider. Meanwhile Mary wears her usual thin-lipped expression as she laboriously sews the diagonal bands of the Neville crest onto the bodice of my gown. At thirty years, she is already old, married to Papa's son by his first marriage, Sir Ralph Neville.

> *Which would you have? The choice is all your own.'*
> *The knight thought long, and with a piteous groan*
> *At last he said, with all the care in life,*
> *'My lady and my love, my dearest wife,*
> *I leave the matter to your wise decision.*
> *You make the choice yourself, for the provision*
> *Of what may be agreeable and rich*
> *In honor to us both, I don't care which;*
> *Whatever pleases you, suffices me.'*
> *'And have I won the mastery?' said she,*
> *'Since I'm to choose and rule as I think fit?'*
> *'Certainly, wife,' he answered her, 'that's it.'*

Anne puts her sewing down and frowns. Four years older than me at thirteen, she's expecting her first child, being married to the Earl of Stafford. "You mean," she says, "his wife rules him? But how can that be, Mother?"

"What kind of woman was the knight's wife?" asks Mama, turning to Anne.

I cannot contain myself. "She was the one who told him the answer to that riddle, Mama. She told him that what a woman most desires is sovereignty. She wants to rule her own life, her husband, and her lover."

Mary looks up and frowns. I toss my head, and smile. Mary is always sour, always quick to find fault, always hard to please.

But Mama's lips quirk at the corners as she shakes her head at me and says, "Let Anne respond, my love." She turns to Anne. "How would you describe her?"

"She was very well read," says Anne, slowly. "She quoted Dante, Catullus and Juvenal. So she could read Italian and Latin. Perhaps the knight, her husband, let her make the decisions because she was so wise."

"But is education the same as wisdom?" asks Mama.

Anne is silent while I look around. The late September afternoon sunlight is bright on the round carpet of Mama's solar. It is peaceful here, away from the swirling winds outside. A bee hums. Silken threads whisper as Mary and Jenet pull their needles through the velvet. A spoon tinkles against glass as my eldest sister Cath, visiting from the estates of her husband, the Duke of Norfolk, stirs a distillation of rose petals. I yawn, and quickly bend over the tunic I am embroidering, a betrothal present for Richard. I've selected purple velvet to betoken his royal blood, while embroidering the hem in a pattern of songbirds. The yellow thread makes their song bright and cheerful.

"No," says Anne at last. "But it helps to develop your mind, to give you discernment, to learn to discriminate."

"Indeed it does, my love," says Mama, patting her hand.

I cover another yawn. I'll fall asleep soon if nothing interesting happens. I put my sewing down, get up, and pour a cup of wine for Cath. It might make her talkative. Though past twenty-seven, she seems young because so merry.

"Cath," I say. "Did Queen Alainor of Aquitaine have great learning?"

Catrine, named after our mother's mother, Catrine de Roet, sips her wine quickly, loving to talk about the past. "That's not what made her so famous. When she was married to King Louis, they went off on crusade together, and Queen Alainor and all her ladies dressed as Amazons. They wore breastplates, carried swords, and rode like men."

"And what about King Louis? Was he dashing?"

"He was dressed as a monk and walked a great deal of the way."

I am crushed that my heroine should have to put up with someone like that. He sounds worse than Richard. "They seem rather ill-sorted," I say. Cath bursts out laughing.

"That marriage didn't last long," she remarks. "Once Alainor got her divorce from Louis, she married Henry of Anjou, who was thirteen years younger—"

"Thirteen years younger?" I gape at her. "A younger husband? I didn't think that was allowed."

"Cath!" says Mary. "That's enough. You shouldn't fill Cis's head with such ideas." She turns to me. "Pick up your embroidery, child; you have much to do so it is suitable for Richard to wear."

I absently finger the tunic before me. A much younger husband would not even be born yet, for I am only nine—

"Mary," says Mama. "Cecylee knows her duty."

"Not as well as Anne," says Mary, her lips thinning.

This is true. Anne sits there, quietly sewing. I don't know how she does it. How can you concentrate on something as dull as embroidery, when all these tales are inviting you to imagine all sorts of things? I eye Richard's tunic and turn to Mama. "Is it true that a woman may marry only once?"

"That depends on canon law," replies Mama.

"Bishops and the church determine that?" asks Anne.

"Men! Men always do!" I exclaim.

Mama takes some time to explain what canon law is. I pick up Richard's tunic. Perhaps it would be well to finish it soon, so I can make something pretty for myself.

"It's ridiculous, all this talk about canon law," says Audrey under her breath. She sits down beside me and threads her needle with silver thread. "I ask you, most women are lucky if they manage to survive one husband, with all those pregnancies, let alone several. Men always want the same thing." She bites off the silver thread with the one tooth that is left in the side of her mouth. "They don't always stop to think if their favorite sport is good for their young brides. Look at Lady Anne. She was only twelve when she married the Duke of Buckingham last year, and now she's expecting her first child at thirteen."

I look up to see Mama's reaction. But she talks as if nothing has happened: "Most people don't worry about remarrying nowadays. You can marry as often as you please—provided that your husbands are dead first." She smiles at me, then turns to Anne. "Which women have power?"

"Abbesses," says Anne. "They may ride out of their convents and conduct business with important men."

"Widows with rank and money," I put in quickly. "Once your husband is dead, you may do as you please. You can manage your land, plead lawsuits, spend your own money." I throw back my head and peal with laughter, contemplating the luxury of so much freedom.

"Makes you wonder why more husbands are not bumped off," says Audrey, "when wealthy widows have much more power than rich wives."

A hush descends. Anne and Jenet stare, their needles suspended in mid air. Mama bites her lip. Catrine looks amused. Mary stands. "My lady mother, how can you countenance this? If you do not curb her, Cecylee will imagine she can do as she pleases."

"You're too hard on her, Mary," says Catrine.

"Life is going to be hard on Cecylee," replies Mary. "You know she has no choice in the matter of her husband."

"I am well aware of that," says Mama, flushing. "But I see no reason why Cecylee may not enjoy the girlhood that is left to her."

"My lady mother, your judgment is usually faultless, but you are blind about Cecylee," continues Mary.

Mama rises. "You know the sacrifices I have been forced to make."

"How can you expect her to be a dutiful wife?"

"I never see Bess, my eldest, because she lives on the other side of the mountains."

"Filling her head with the Wife of Bath only makes things worse."

"I never see Jehane, because she is a nun."

"You never say no to her."

"Alainor is lost to me because she is married to the heir of our worst enemy, Henry Percy, Earl of Northumberland."

"Cecylee is acquiring a temper to go along with her haughty ways."

"Anne and Catrine must live with their husbands and can make only rare visits."

"And you do not see this, because she winds you around her finger as if she were reeling in a day's catch."

"And the only reason why I see you, Mary, is because you are married to a Neville and live at Castle Raby."

"You're so jealous—" says Catrine, and then stops.

The unmistakable sound of mail-shod feet climbs the spiral staircase. It sends prickles up the spine. Quick as a flash of steel, Cath bundles Master Chaucer's manuscripts into a chest and shuts the lid.

"Mama—" says Anne. But Mama takes my hand and says, "If it's the last thing I do, I'll not be parted from my Cecylee."

Papa enters the solar.

Mama grips my hand tight.

Papa narrows his eyes. "Well, my lady?"

Mama draws herself up. "You agreed that Cecylee could visit me in Bulmer's Tower—"

"What's this I hear about never being parted from Cecylee?"

I flick my gaze from Papa to Mama. "Mama means that she would like me to visit more often."

Papa fingers his beard as he glances at me. He gives a harsh bark of laughter. "So be it!" he exclaims. "Provided you include young Richard in your visits." He strides to the door and turns. "It would do the lad good to spend more time with the ladies, do you not agree, madam?" And laughing, he pounds down the stairs, his mailed foot striking each stone step.

Mama's fingers clutch mine as we both sweep him a low curtsey.

Chapter 3
Feast of Saint Luke
October 18, 1424

My eyes snap open.

The day of my betrothal; my stomach spasms into knots.

Why be betrothed now? At nine I'm expected to enter a woman's estate, with a woman's cares and responsibilities. Where is my girlhood? I don't want it to end. I'm comfortable with Mama and enjoy my studies. I don't see why all of this can't continue.

Maybe I can delay things.

The door opens. Jenet pours warmed water into a bowl and hands over a linen napkin to dry my hands and face. She stokes the fire into a blaze before helping me into a fur-lined robe. I put my feet into fur-lined slippers, Jenet wraps her red woolen mantle tight, and then we file onto the wooden walkway for our cold and invigorating walk around the kitchen tower to the chapel.

A crisp cold morning, the sunlight cuts through the golden leaves of the trees. Smoke curls lazily from the castle kitchens where servants labor to prepare the betrothal feast. As we emerge from the staircase into the chapel, the deep bell tolls, calling people to early morning Mass.

Today, a large crowd gathers, my kinfolk having ridden into Castle Raby to take part in the celebrations. As I enter the chapel, I catch a glimpse of my eldest brother Richard Neville, Baron Montacute, who has twenty-four years. He stands at the front of the chapel with Alice Montacute, his sixteen-year-old wife. They've spent the last month traveling 300 miles from their estates in the south of England, bringing with them their baby Cecily, named in honor of me.

I look around. My two half-sisters, four sisters, and several brothers are all in attendance. My betrothal to Richard is part of a double ceremony, for my seven-year-old baby

brother Edward will marry a wealthy heiress and bear the title
Lord Bergavenny in right of his wife. His wife-to-be, Lady
Lisbet de Beauchamp, stands next to him. She has a pale face,
pale pink lips, pale hair, and pale blue eyes. She stands very
still. You would not think to look at her that she is my age.
Edward is two years younger, so she is lucky enough to get a
young husband she can boss around.

  After Mass, I go back to my apartment in the keep,
accompanied by Jenet, who has to wash and dress me and do
my hair. I am so busy concocting my plan I don't notice the
ladies gathering to greet me. A well-known voice makes me
jump.
  "Cecylee, sweeting, guess what I have for you."
  "Cath." I exclaim. "I'm busy—"
  "Listen to her Impatience, the next Duchess of
York."
  I blush.
  "Don't you want to know?" she cajoles, hiding
something behind her back.
  I sigh and resist stamping my foot. Bother Cath for
getting in the way.
  "What is it?"
  "You have to guess."
  I close my eyes as I rack my brains. Why does Cath
have to be so irritating? "A mirror," say I, guessing wildly.
  "My baby sister is as cunning as a fox!" exclaims Cath
as she brandishes the object in front of me. I focus my eyes
on something very bright that reflects the light. It *is* a mirror,
a beautiful silver mirror with a matching silver comb. Both
have sinuous decorations on the handles and edges, my name
carved discreetly within. I am struck dumb.
  "Really, Catrine!" exclaims Mama, a twinkle in her eye.
"You encourage Cecylee to be vain."
  I look up. My sisters, half-sisters, sisters-by-marriage,
their maids and other female relatives fill the apartments. As
the laughter dies away the sound of a soft footfall comes, and
Anne appears with Humphrey, her new baby boy, the future

Earl of Stafford. Even though it's now three weeks since the birth of her son, Anne looks pale and has violet shadows under her eyes.

"I'm fine, Mother, truly," she says in response to Mama's unspoken question. "I just tire easily."

"Sit by me and rest." says Mama. She takes the baby from Anne while Cath goes to the kitchens to oversee the refreshments.

Anne sits down, and from her sleeve she produces a small package wrapped up in linen. She smiles at me.

Another present! I unwrap it to find a purse made out of sky blue silk and lined with dark blue damask. My name is embroidered in seed pearls on the front.

"Did you make this?"

Anne nods.

I hold it up. The embroidery is finely wrought with small neat stitches and no knots or threads hanging loose—so different from my own travails, so perfect.

I give it to Mama; she examines it with gentle fingers.

"You can take that to the fair," says Anne, "with money in it from Richard to buy yourself some luxuries."

My cheeks warm. Even my quiet sister Anne has noticed Richard's attentions, how he always presents me with tokens of his affection like sewing scissors, thimbles, and needles—things I need for the everlasting embroidery I am supposed to do. When the fair comes, he buys me headbands, snoods, veils, hair-pins, earrings, and necklaces. I delight in these presents, but should I really accept them?

"It is beautiful," says Mama, kissing Anne's cheek. "How you found the time to do it when you had to ready yourself for your first child I do not know. Cecylee, my love, thank your sister."

I hug my sister tight as Mama wipes tears away with her fingers.

More company arrives in the shape of Richard's fifteen-year-old sister Isabel, married to Sir Thomas Grey. Mama greets her, trying to prompt a smile from her sad face, and settles down to gossip with the ladies who now preen themselves in front of their mirrors.

I tiptoe away.

When I reappear some time later, I am just in time to see the women from the kitchen struggling up the stairs with buckets of warm water. Jenet tests the temperature of the water with her elbow, then helps me out of my clothing, and I step into the tub. She washes my hair in rosemary soap, then tenderly smoothes an oily paste made of finely ground almonds onto my skin to cleanse it, washing it off with angelica water. After that, she helps me out of the tub and dries me off.

With her help, I put on silk stockings and tie the garters just above the knee. When I stand, I hold my arms so that Jenet can pull the ivory silk chemise over my head. Then Jenet can braid my hair into plaits. She coils the plaits around my head, pins them, and then carefully covers her handiwork with a hair net.

As I relax under Jenet's gentle ministrations, the door bangs and Audrey appears.

"My lady," she says to Mama, "I cannot find Lady Cecylee's gown. I swear I had it with me this last hour and now it's disappeared." She turns to Thomasina, Cath's maid, and Gunilda, Anne's maid. "Don't just stand there. Help me find it. Search your ladies' things."

A hubbub ensues. I smile as I calculate how long this will keep everyone busy. I find a quiet corner, fold my hands, and keep my eyes downcast. I count things; trees, sheep, ospreys. I am just getting started on castles, when I sense someone standing in front of me. I glance up and see Anne.

"Cis," she whispers, "where is it?"

"Where is what?" I ask.

"You know what I mean," whispers Anne. "Where have you hidden your gown?"

"I haven't," I say.

Anne opens her mouth to say something when the door opens. Cath reappears, followed by servants bearing food on trays and cups of wine. There are pies made out of game, several different kinds of cheese, round flat rolls of manchet bread, mead and hippocras, a spicy wine.

The servants put the food down and withdraw while Cath takes in the crowd of women surrounding Mama, gesticulating and wailing over the disappearance of my gown. Her eyes flick over to me. She beckons.

I make my way slowly over, clenching my hands as she fixes me with a firm look. "Stop playing games," she hisses. "You cannot hurt Mama in this way—"

"In what way?" I say.

"I know you've hidden it, you little prankster," Cath continues, her voice rising. "Where is it?"

She says it in such a loud voice, it reaches to the ends of the earth. Everyone has heard everything and the room grows quiet. The weight of many eyes fall on me, their expressions a mixture of exasperation, pity, amusement, and disappointment. I flush to the roots of my hair.

The silence holds. Then the door opens and Mary appears.

"I found this in my bedchamber, concealed in my garderobe," she says, shaking out the bundle in her arms to reveal the missing gown. She glares at me. "Someone must have put it there by mistake."

I twist my hands, hang my head. Mary's the dressmaker of the family, and I thought I could conveniently hide my gown amongst everyone else's finery.

"*Cecylee!*" says Mama. Just that one word, but it makes me cringe with shame.

The room rustles as remarks fly.

"Such wild manners," whispers the Countess of Warwick to her neighbor. "I would never let my daughter behave in that way."

Mama reddens and bites her lip.

"Let me," says Anne, taking the dress from Mary and smoothing it out. "I'm already dressed, so I can help Cecylee."

With Anne helping, Jenet slowly brings the heavy velvet, midnight-blue betrothal gown over my head. They lace it up at the sides and attach the triangular sleeves over my long-sleeved chemise. Jenet places the blue velvet head-roll on my head and pins on the translucent silken veil. Anne helps me into the shoes, pointed poulaines made of matching dark blue velvet with the Neville crest on top.

The dress is ablaze in silver embroidery. There is the Neville crest at my bodice, and the bullion knots on the skirts give way to a silver, flowery mead with horned sheep. At the bottom around the hem is embroidered *Cecylee, Duchesse of Yorke*.

I am ready.

The gentlemen rise and bow as Mama and I enter the great hall followed by the ladies. On that never-to-be-forgotten morning, the great hall looks magnificent, decorated with apples, autumn roses and sheaves of corn. The lighted wax tapers make the stone walls and silverware glow, and new rushes of meadowsweet give off a sweet scent of newly cut hay and flowers.

Cardinal Beaufort, Mama's younger brother, clears his throat. "We are met here today, to witness the betrothal of Richard Plantagenet, Duke of York, to Lady Cecylee de Neville."

Richard smiles at me. I ignore him, staring instead at the finely embroidered handkerchief placed into my hands by Mama.

Cardinal Beaufort raises his voice. "If there be any among you who know why Richard, Duke of York, and Lady Cecylee de Neville may not be betrothed, say you so now, or forever hold your peace."

I look around. Surely someone will say something. They do not.

Cardinal Beaufort turns to me. "My child," he says, "do you consent to this betrothal?"

I tense. I look at Papa, and he nods. I look at Mama. She nods also.

"Yes," I murmur, looking down.

Cardinal Beaufort turns to Richard. "Duke Richard, take you Lady Cecylee's hands."

Richard's warm and moist hands take mine. I make a supreme effort not to snatch them away. While Cardinal Beaufort speaks the words that bind us to marry at some future date, I stare at my blue velvet slippers. I don't look at Richard until Cardinal Beaufort is in the middle of marrying little Edward to Lady Lisbet.

"Does this mean I don't have to be locked up any more?"

Richard stares at me. He draws himself up. "You must stay in your apartments."

I set my lips into a line.

"I may be King of England one day."

"I hate being locked up because of you."

Richard flinches. "Cecylee," he says, "calm yourself. I am here to protect you."

"I don't want your protection," I mutter, looking away.

"One day you will be my wife."

"But I don't want to be your wife if I have to be locked up like a caged animal."

"I am the heir to the throne."

"I hate these chains!"

"You must do what your lord father tells you."

"I want to be free!"

"Cis!" A deep bellow casts a pall.

I freeze.

Papa strides up, putting his hands on his hips and glaring at me. "Well?" he says. "What do you have to say?"

I do not know what to say. Truly, my lord father and I do not see eye-to-eye on this matter.

"My lord, it is nothing," stammers Richard.

Papa shakes his head. "Lord Richard, you are too kind. Mark my words, you will be ill recompensed for being so. Cecylee must learn to bear the consequences of her actions."

I lift my head. "I told him I did not want to be locked up."

"And why are you locked up?" asks Papa softly.

"I don't know," I murmur.

"Speak up, my lady."

"I don't know."

Papa grasps me by the arm. "Don't you? Then I shall have to teach you, my fine lady. Until then, you will show the company that you know how to behave. Is that understood?"

I look at the floor, moisten my lips.

"Is that understood?" thunders Papa.

I flinch. "Yes, my lord father."

He glares at me.

I sweep him a low curtsey.

He stalks off.

Richard lets out a long breath. "Are you affrighted, Cis?"

"No."

"Isn't he going to punish you?"

I am silent.

"You have greatly angered him—"

With a flourish of trumpets, the food arrives in a procession of platters set down first on the high table, then on the lower tables. Silently, Richard takes my hand and leads me to the place of honor in the middle of the high table.

The feast begins with thick turnip soup, flat manchet bread, and goat cheese; platters of green beans, sweet peas, and carrots follow. There is pike stuffed with a mixture of breadcrumbs and herbs. While the dishes are being cleared away, the first sugar sculpture is presented, created by Audrey's son. On one platter is Castle Raby with a rose in front of it, to honor me, the Rose of Raby. On the other platter is a white lion to symbolize Richard, who has taken the White Lion of March as his personal badge in honor of his late mother, Lady Anne de Mortimer.

At another flourish from the trumpets, the meat course arrives. There is a Swan and a Boar's Head with an orange in its mouth, followed by a large piece of beef dressed with rosemary and sage. At the end of the procession, servants carry silver sauce boats, salt cellars and pipes of wine.

The feast ends with another subtlety of the *Lady and the Unicorn*. The Unicorn bears an unmistakable resemblance to Richard, showing him sitting docilely at my feet. Richard reddens upon recognizing himself. But roars of laughter from Papa and the applause of the guests mask his embarrassment; everyone rises and drinks our health. The minstrels strike up a lively air, and Richard leads me into the hall for the first dance. How I love to dance! I even manage a smile for Richard.

At last afternoon melts into evening, and Mama takes me by the hand. We bid our guests a "God go with you" and leave.

I don't have to wait long. I'm sitting by the fire with Audrey in attendance, dressed only in my chemise, when Papa strides up to my room, birch twigs in hand. He makes me bend over and lifts my skirts. The twigs cut into my bare skin. I try not to cry out, but soon give up.

I am furious.

Why shouldn't I be free?

Why should I be forced to marry someone I don't want?

I hate Richard.

I hate my lord father.

I hate men.

I will never forgive them.

Never. Never. Never. Never.

Never. Never. Never.

Never.

Never.

Chapter 4
Feast of Saint Ursula & The Blessed Virgins
October 21, 1425

I bring the pony to a stop. Before me, sprawled on the ground, lies my lord father, Ralph de Neville, the Earl of Westmorland. His right leg sticks out at a funny angle. Next to him kneels Richard. He is weeping.

"Help me off," I say.

We've been riding from Sheriff Hutton to Middleham to transact business and collect revenues. I have been allowed to come along, accompanied, naturally, by Richard. We ride in the middle of the party, surrounded by knights, when we hear a sudden shout. I dig my heels into Doucette to make her go faster, but the docile little pony merely snorts and continues at her customary pace while Richard's gelding surges to the front of the line.

I disengage myself from Richard and stand over my father. Is he dead? I stare at him hard, but he doesn't move.

A thunder of hooves reverberates, and my brother Salisbury vaults off his horse. Instantly, everyone doffs their hats and kneels.

Father is dead.

Salisbury motions everyone up and stands beside Richard. "Did you see him go down?"

Richard shakes his head.

"He clutched his chest, grimaced, and tumbled off," says Sir Ralph Neville the Older, riding up. Sir Ralph is one of father's numerous younger sons by his first marriage, thus my half-brother.

Salisbury bends over and places a stubby finger on father's forehead. "He's as cold as marble," he mutters. He fishes two golden sovereigns out of his leather pouch and places them over the lids to close them. Then he straightens up and gives orders for father to be borne to Castle Raby.

I stand still, looking at father. He doesn't move. I stare at the fallen leaves on the ground, then lift my eyes to the huge oak tree that stands in my path. It has been blasted by a summer storm and is dead. Underneath it are the green shoots of new trees. Papa is like that oak, sheltering us from storms. What will become of us now? What of Mama? Will she have anything, or will she be forced to beg like those old women I see by the edge of the road when I ride my pony into Staindrop?

"He's already acting as heir!" exclaims Sir Ralph.

I look up.

Sir Ralph clutches the reins, causing his stallion to prance.

"I thought he was," says Richard.

"Well, you thought wrong," snaps Sir Ralph, swinging his stallion around. "My nephew and namesake is heir. I must ride to Brancepeth and tell him so before that upstart takes more than is his right." He digs his knees in, and the stallion bounds off across the desolate moorland.

I stare after the rapidly fading figure of Sir Ralph Neville the Older, the cold wind snapping my veil. I am ten years old. It is just over a year since I was forced into that betrothal with Richard. The seasons have rolled around, bringing in the bright, chill days of October.

What does this mean? I know, of course, that Sir Ralph is my father's second son by his first marriage. Sir Ralph's elder brother, Sir John Neville, died some five years ago, and so Sir John's eldest son, Sir Ralph Neville the Younger, stands to inherit.

Or does he?

What about brother Salisbury? He is the eldest son of my father's second marriage to Mama, Joan de Beaufort, and father has always treated him as the heir. Salisbury has royal blood flowing in his veins like me, for our mother's father, John of Gaunt, was son to King Edward III.

Has father actually gone against English law and custom and disinherited the children of his first marriage?

"Where's he gone?"

I turn to see Salisbury standing there.

"Brancepeth," says Richard.

"Aye, he would," mutters Salisbury, flicking mud off his blue velvet tunic. "We have not a moment to lose." He claps his hands. "We ride to Raby."

"To Raby!" shout the men in response.

I follow Richard as he strides beside Salisbury into the great hall of Castle Raby. They bow before the high table, where Mama presides in state. Before her stands a tall young man I do not recognize.

"He's already here," mutters Salisbury.

The stranger turns, and I draw breath, for Sir Ralph Neville the Younger is the veritable image of my lord father. Salisbury smiles and takes the new Earl of Westmorland by the elbow. "Congratulations, my lord, on your new title." He looks meaningfully at the servants. The entire household rises to its feet, and the steward proposes a toast.

"Wass-hail," they roar. "May you have good health." A great noise fills the hall as they clank cups and goblets, precious metal, clay, and pewter, to drink to the new earl.

The second Earl of Westmorland flushes with pleasure and rubs his hands as he looks around the handsome old hall. His gaze lights on me. "Is this little Cis?"

I make my curtsey.

"Yes, my lord," says Mama. She makes a small gesture in the direction of Richard. "Are you acquainted with my lord of York, her betrothed?"

Richard inclines his head. Sir Ralph makes a perfunctory bow in return and continues to stare at me. I lift my chin, a flush mounting into my cheeks.

The new earl chuckles. He turns to Salisbury. "When do you and your lady mother leave for Bisham Manor?"

The great hall grows silent as Salisbury narrows his eyes. At last, he says: "I thought you knew—"

"Knew what?" snaps Westmorland.

"I thought you knew that your grandfather left most of his lands to my lady mother."

I glance at Mama.

"No!" roars Westmorland. "I am the heir of the late earl's eldest son. These lands are mine by the laws of England."

Salisbury beckons to his scribe. "Show my lord of Westmorland a copy of his late grandfather's will."

Westmorland glances at it, then balls the document between his fists. "God's teeth!" he explodes. "I am to be Earl in name only!"

"You get Brancepeth," says Salisbury.

"Aye, but Castle Raby, Sheriff Hutton, and Middleham with all their vast holdings go to that—" he breaks off abruptly and flushes.

"They go to my lady mother," says Salisbury.

"Which you get when she dies."

"I do not think we should be talking of the death of my lady mother."

"As if you don't have enough land, with all those rich holdings in the south your wife brought you when you married."

"My lord father did not want my lady mother to be destitute."

"And what do I get? Nothing, except for Brancepeth and a few paltry manors in the north of this country on poor land."

"You are the Earl of Westmorland."

The new earl glares, his blue eyes looking as icy as his grandfather's. He stalks out of the hall.

There is silence for a few moments, then conversations rumble.

Richard turns to Salisbury. "What do you suppose he'll do?"

Salisbury sighs. "I know not. But we haven't seen the end of this."

"He'll go to the Percies to seek their aid in taking our land," says Mama. "I heard he plans to marry Lady Elizabeth Percy."

"But she's old enough to be his mother!" says Salisbury.

Mama purses her lips and shrugs.

"I must see to our defenses." Salisbury bows and leaves.

Richard glances at me, but I take my place beside Mama. Richard looks around the room, as if seeking someone, then bows to Mama and leaves.

Mama puts down her knife and draws a handkerchief from her sleeve. I see that she is weeping.

"Mama," I say softly.

She takes my hand and attempts a weak smile.

"Papa?"

She nods. "Your brother tells me he didn't suffer." She gulps. "But I miss him so. I can't believe he's no longer here."

"But—" I don't quite know how to put this. "You didn't always agree."

She brushes her tears away and takes me gently by the shoulders: "Understand this, my love, your father and I were the best of friends."

"But—"

"Of course, we didn't always agree. You'll understand when you're a married lady yourself."

I frown.

She leans forward and whispers. "Look what he did for me. He left me everything of value in his will."

I look at her, and it is as if everything becomes lighter. I smile.

Mama smiles back.

"My lady!" The steward appears, bowing. He engages Mama in a long discussion.

I pick at my food, but can't eat. Suddenly, the hall seems unbearably hot and stuffy. I long to get outside. I want to think about everything Mama has told me. When the steward has gone, I lean forward. "Mama," I say. "It's such a glorious day. May I ride out on Doucette?"

Mama nods absently.

I rise, filled with sudden energy. After a year of being mewed up in the castle keep, I will be alone.

I run.

I run with a speed I didn't know I had, my heart pounding in my chest.

I don't know where I get the energy, for I haven't run in such a long time.

I head for Bulmer's Tower and fly up the stairs towards Mama's bedchamber. I fling myself onto her bed, gasping and sobbing.

Audrey appears. "My lady Cecylee. Whatever has happened?" She takes me by the shoulders. "Why, child, you are a sight to behold, your headdress gone, your hair wild, your clothes torn—" She pales. "Did someone try—?"

I nod, unable to speak.

"Who?"

"The new earl," I manage to gasp out.

It is nearing dusk by the time brother Salisbury returns, followed by Richard and a large party of men— mostly untrained recruits carrying pitchforks, shovels and other farm implements.

I doze in Mama's bed, dressed in a clean silk chemise. I've been given a bath, my bruises and scrapes treated with a salve. Mama strokes my hair and tells me I've been very brave, that I did right to run away. She promises she'll take care of matters, that I should worry no more.

I gaze at her, unable to speak, tears sliding down my cheeks. I can feel his slimy hands cup my breasts, smell his foul breath on my cheek. Every time I think of it, I shiver violently and retch into a bucket.

Mail-shod feet pound up the stairs. Audrey opens the door a crack and drops a deep curtsey. Mama rises from her place on the window seat, taking Salisbury into an adjoining room.

Eventually Salisbury leaves. I hear him speaking to someone outside: "My lady mother wishes to see you." Then I hear the bang, bang, bang of feet going downstairs.

There is silence for a while, then Richard's voice fills the room. "I am more sorry than I can say about the death of your lord husband."

"I dare say you are."

Silence. I hear the rustle of parchment, as if someone is searching for something.

"We came back as soon as we could, madam."

Silence. More rustling. A chair scrapes. "I hold you responsible for Lady Cecylee's safety. It is your duty to protect her."

"But Cis does not welcome my visits."

"Why did you leave?"

"To help Salisbury raise his men."

"Did you not notice the way Westmorland stared at her?"

Dead silence.

"I thought you hadn't noticed."

"Did he not ride to Alnwick?"

"I had no men to spare to see that my daughter was safe."

"I thought it made sense to help Salisbury with his levies."

"If her hound had not bitten Westmorland, Lady Cecylee would have been ruined."

"Ruined?"

"I am saying she would have been forced to marry him."

"Marry him? But I thought he was going to marry Lady Elizabeth!"

"Are you so doltish you could not see what his game was?"

Silence.

"He could have demanded Castle Raby and the other manors as her dowry. And we would have been unable to refuse."

I am a pawn in the greedy and unscrupulous hands of men. I lean over the bucket and retch up the rest of my dinner.

"If you want Lady Cecylee, impress me. Show me you are truly worthy."

"I am a Plantagenet, the Duke of York."

"An empty title. Where are your lands? Held by the Crown. Because your father was executed as a traitor."

"But I have been promised my lands back once I reach my majority."

"You're only fourteen now. That's seven years away."

I hear a crackle, someone opening a document.

"I will continue to hold your wardship, but I think you should reside with your brother-in-law."

"I will go to Sir Thomas Grey directly," says Richard. "But in the matter of my wardship, I beg you not to break my betrothal to Cecylee. I consider the promise I made that day a sacred vow."

"You are not married to Cecylee. I made sure of that."

"I would like to see Lady Cecylee, to bid her farewell."

My heart drops into my stomach. I'm so ill, I'll humiliate myself in front of him.

"You are not yet worthy." Mama's voice shines into the darkened room: "No."

Chapter 5
Bisham Manor, Berkshire
April to May 1437

On the death of my lord father, the marriage negotiations fell into the hands of Salisbury. Fortunately for me, brother Salisbury is more at home commanding his soldiers than persuading Mama to discuss my marriage, so he doesn't try too hard to press Richard's case. Enjoying a girlhood my sisters never had, every May for the next eleven years I set off with Mama and Salisbury into the north of the country to manage our vast estates in Yorkshire and Westmorland. We go with a heavily armed escort, for the new Earl of Westmorland continues to feud over the Middleham estates and the Percies make occasional raids. Every October, we return south to Bisham Manor to spend Christmas with Salisbury's wife, Alice, and their growing family.

Alice and other ladies of my age and status grow old and ill as they birth one child after another. Still I have no husband. Yet while this makes me sigh with relief, thanks to father, I'm styled Duchess of York and am always announced as such. I haven't seen Richard in eleven years, and with leisure, I ponder: What should I do with my life?

The answer comes from an unexpected quarter. Now that Mama spends half of the year at Bisham Manor in the south of England, the abbess of Barking Abbey makes it her business to call frequently upon her half-sister. Abbess Margaret de Swynford travels with several nuns in her train and is kind enough to bring her cousin Elizabeth Chaucer and her half-niece Lady Jehane de Neville with her. And so Mama is able to see a niece, as well as a daughter she believed to be lost.

Lady Jehane, my long-lost sister, has cultivated an air of quietude that draws others to her. She listens attentively as I tell her about my dilemma.

"Richard is not a bad person," I say. "I think he's fond of me, or was. But I don't love him, and I don't think he could make me happy. Indeed, my whole being revolts at the idea of being tied down in marriage."

"There's no reason why you couldn't take the veil."

"But I couldn't leave Mama."

"Of course not. She has set much store by you, her youngest daughter." Lady Jehane gives me a smile, untinged with bitterness. "But one day, Our Blessed Lady will gather our lady mother into her arms. If you're not married by then, you could take the veil. I would help you."

My soul soars. I would be spared the rigors of childbearing. I would have opportunities few other women dream of. I could cultivate my mind and improve my handwriting and my grasp of languages. I could learn to make medicines. I could lead a life of quiet contemplation.

I would have a measure of freedom.

But Richard achieved his majority in 1432, obtaining his vast estates back from the Crown. He became the wealthiest peer in the land. Then, in 1436, the king's council decided that Richard of York should replace the king's uncle as governor of Normandy and regent of France, the Duke of Bedford dying unexpectedly at the age of forty-six.

Becoming governor of Normandy was quite a coup for a young man of twenty-four, but it was not a coup for me as Richard now pressed his suit with more vigor and persistence. In April 1437, he even returned to England from Normandy.

Now, he demands to see me.

I recoil.

I remember well how my lord father gave me a beating after I'd dared to question his right to lock me up. I have the scars to prove it. The last time any man touched me was when Sir Ralph Neville lifted my skirts in the stables at Castle Raby. Even now, that humiliation makes me shudder.

The world of men is filled with violence, and I want none of it.

I am seated on a low stool, singing softly, surrounded by brother Salisbury's children, when the crunch of gravel reaches my ears. Looking up, I find a young man.

He is well dressed in rich hues of velvet, as befits a noble. He fingers his heavy gold collar, decorated with white roses done in enamel. From this showy bijou drops a huge spear-pointed diamond.

A prickle wends it way up my spine. There is a silence as he stares at me.

"Need you something, my lord?" I enquire.

Absently fingering the diamond, the young man stutters out a reply. "My lady Cecylee—forgive this intrusion —I see you know not who I am." He takes a deep breath. "Remember you a boy named Richard?"

God have mercy upon my soul. I look down at my lap. I had better get this over with, and quickly. I look up, and lock eyes.

He reads my face hungrily, as if concerned about my feelings. Then he smiles. His smile transforms his face, lighting up his blue-grey eyes and imbuing his expression with warmth and delight.

I cannot help it, I smile back. "Richard, it is you!" I exclaim. "Only you look different. I had not expected to see you look like—"

"Like what, sweetheart? You mean old and ugly?"

I tilt my head as I take him in. "There is a different feel about you." I frown, trying to reconcile the serious, rather pompous boy I'd known with this attractive young man who kneels before me. Then I blush. What am I thinking? I do not wish to marry.

"I see my intrusion has discomforted you, my sweeting, for the which I am sorry. I should not have come upon you this way."

I graze him with a glance. Is he making fun of me?

"We promised once to marry, my lady, but I'd not force you to it against your will."

Now I stare.

He leans forward. "Is it still your wish to be my wife?"

I thin my lips and veil my eyes with my lashes. So this is why brother Salisbury has been closeted inside all morning. They must have been signing the marriage papers. Naturally, no one bothered to inform me.

I rise. "You know me not, my lord," I say. Then I sweep out of the garden.

I go to Mama. I do not have to say anything, for she takes one look at my face and nods.

I am gone within the hour.

A message reaches me at vespers the next day: my lord of York arrived to pay a visit but was turned away. He will return in a week.

I smile and toss the note into the flames.

A week later, at the appointed time, Richard, Duke of York, claims admittance to Barking Abbey, where I enjoy the hospitality of Abbess Margaret de Swynford. Lady Jehane has kept me company during this time, and I have attended every Holy Office. I find the quiet darkness of the church where the nuns murmur their prayers soothing to my spirits.

I will tell Richard no, then stay here and take the veil.

I sit in my chamber when he appears. The windows face out onto Abbess Margaret's herb garden. The scent of rosemary and sage fill the room. Audrey and Jenet sit in a corner, engaged in sewing. I read a book in Latin, making notes about it in French.

Richard stares at this scene while I turn to my book.

"How did you learn Latin?" he asks, sitting down beside me without invitation.

"While I waited for you to return, I decided to educate myself," I reply. "My brother Edward was learning Latin, so I begged my lady mother to let me sit in on his classes. Eventually, his tutor Doctor Eusebius agreed to take me on as his pupil."

"I see," says Richard. His eyes strain to look at the title of the book on the table. I give it to him to examine. It is Boethius's *Consolation of Philosophy*. He stares at me. "Do you like philosophy?"

"It makes you think hard about things," I say. "It is very consoling in times of crisis."

I put that book down and open another. Again, Richard cranes his neck. I hold it up for him to see. *The City of Ladies* by Christine de Pizan.

Richard's eyebrows lift as if he's never allowed that a woman could write a book.

"Christine de Pizan was a learned lady, highly regarded by the Queen of France," I say. "This book is a retelling of history from a woman's point of view." I pause and turn to be sure I have his attention. "Have you noticed that history is always told from a man's point of view?" I smile. There.

He stares back but does not recoil. "Cecylee, you are full of surprises," he finally says. "I never would have guessed that the pert, contrary young lady I used to know has turned into a scholar and an ascetic."

I lower my eyes. "You don't have to marry me if you think it unseemly to have such a well-educated wife—"

I stop, because Richard is kissing me. On the lips. I shudder. No one has ever done this before. I close my eyes; I'm grasped firmly, yet gently; the warmth of his body penetrates my fine woolen gown. At the softness of his lips, I feel myself begin to swoon. "Cis. Don't tease. You know more than anything I want to marry you. But you treat me so badly."

"Don't," I say. "Don't—"

But he kisses me again. I can't help it. His kisses are gentle and respectful, and he holds me softly in his arms. To my surprise, I find myself melting into him.

"You see me for a few hours, then you take fright and rush off in that reckless way you have, forcing me to cool my heels for a week while I'm panting with impatience to see you —"

He sounds like a lover. Does he love me? Is there anything for me in this marriage, apart form an exchange of money and land? "Am I really so difficult?"

"Difficult. You've never been easy. If I weren't madly in love, I'd be tempted to give you a good shaking."

I gaze at him.

He gazes back, his eyes fixed on mine. He looks as if he might care how I feel.

"I'm sorry, Richard," I find myself saying, now calculating. "But I did have to think. It was too much for me after so many years of not seeing you, of not expecting us to marry, of not expecting you to love me or even be very interested."

He should be horrified by this speech. Instead, he looks hurt and—baffled. "How could you think that? I've always been intensely interested in you."

I put my hand on his arm. "Now, Dickon, don't be angry. When my lady mother gave me the girlhood which my sisters never had and I educated myself, many people told me that no gentleman would want to marry me and I'd have to spend my days in a convent."

"But, Cis! You don't understand! I love you! I want your company!"

I give him another hard stare. But he meets it without flinching. He takes my hand and brushes his lips over it. I shiver with pleasure. "Have I now proved to your ladyship's satisfaction that I will be a good and loving husband?"

I come to. He hasn't proved anything. I rise and search through my books. "There is just one more thing."

"One more thing?" His voice mounts higher. "Cis, how much longer do you plan to torture me?" He moves closer and puts an arm around my waist. Again, I feel a pleasurable sensation radiating from his touch. I don't understand it. Surely, after the mistreatment I've met with at the hands of men, I should be dead to amorous advances.

I ignore my feelings, find my book, and say, "Only until you've read this." I hand him *The Wife of Bath's Tale*. "It has some things to say about women, which I would like to discuss with you."

Richard groans but does not lose his temper. Instead, he takes me in his arms and kisses me. "And that will be all? You promise?"

"Promise," I say. If he can swallow that, maybe I should marry him. But I am nearly sure it will enrage him. In which case, I shall refuse him.

Richard sighs. "I don't know why I allow this, but I will read this ... tale and return tomorrow morning." He strokes my cheek with his finger. I close my eyes at the unexpected intimacy of his touch.

The next day Richard reappears. "That's a rather subversive story, Cis."

I look straight at him. "Do you agree with it?"

"You mean that women want to have mastery over their lives in the same way as men? That is what you want me to remember?"

"Yes."

Normally marriage negotiations are handled by my liege lord, my father or brother, without taking my views into account. Yet here I am, twenty-one years old, old enough and well educated enough to act as my own advocate. At this moment I know I have the makings of a ruler, just as Mama said.

I draw myself up. "Remember, Richard, I have a soul to keep. That is why the church allows women to give or *refuse* their consent to marriage. It is important to me that my soul be well matched to that of my husband. Women are not things. We do not want to be viewed as good only for making babies. It is insulting to our intelligence and to our feelings to be treated thus."

Richard's mouth opens, horrified.

I experience a moment of disappointment. But after all, he is a man. What did I expect?

"Cis!" he stutters.

I stare into the abbess's garden as I brace myself for the tirade. I smile.

But Richard does not say anything for a long time. I had forgotten about these silences. I take a deep breath.

"We could make beautiful children," he finally says.

I whirl around and glare at him.

He takes a step backward.

I fold my arms tight across my body. "I do not wish for a lord and vassal relationship. I want you to love me as your equal."

"But haven't I given you every reason to believe that?"

"I have to give up all my legal rights to be your wife."

"You would be Duchess of York."

"What would you do if I displeased you?"

"A marriage vow is a sacred obligation."

"Women have the dice loaded against them."

"Cis!"

"Every time a woman has a child, she goes to the gates of death."

"What are you saying?"

"To please her husband, she is usually required to have one child after another, which is bad for her health."

"Do you take me for a brute?"

"If she displeases him, he can take away her children and lock her up."

"Do you expect me to ride roughshod over your feelings?"

I stare at him. Yes, I do expect him to ride roughshod over my feelings. But something about the way he looks at me prevents me from saying so. Instead, I merely remark, "I don't know you."

"We have known one another since childhood!"

"We have not seen each other in twelve years."

"That was not my wish. I always wanted to see you."

I twist my hands together. I can hear the longing in his voice.

"My love, I think you worry too much. No one could love you as much as I. You must know I don't want a caged animal for a wife, but someone to love me."

I finger my crucifix.

He kneels. "Don't you want to experience the joy of having a husband who loves you?" He takes my hand. "Don't you want to have children to adore?" He kisses my hand and puts it over his heart. "Are you telling me, Cis, that you would prefer to live out your life in your brother's household when I am offering you my hand, my heart, everything I have?"

Unexpected tears come to my eyes. I realize I am wilting through lack of love. A life ruled by prayer now seems colorless and lifeless. All my life, I have spent in my head. The tips of my fingers resonate with each beat of his heart. He kisses each finger of my hand, front and back. The gentle pressure of his touch makes me tingle. I glance at him. He is attractive, lean, muscular, and well dressed. "Come to me, my love," he murmurs, "I adore you. You would be safe with me."

I look away. He sounds hungry for me. What would our wedding night be like? I shiver and close my eyes.

Richard gently kisses each finger. "Would two months give you long enough to get ready?"

Two months? That is not much time. On the other hand, I feel powerful sensations of longing I did not know I possessed.

"Yes—" I sigh out that word on the thread of a whisper, without looking at him, to hide my blushes.

"When?"

I pull myself together and stare at him. "The feast day of Mary Magdalene."

But Richard laughs, his face warming with merriment. "Cis, you really are—"

"Mary Magdalene is much misunderstood," I inform him stiffly.

"My love, of course, if you wish it," he says instantly. He rises and takes my face between his hands. "But have I your promise that we will marry then, in two months time, on the twenty-second day of July, in the Year of Our Lord 1437?"

"On one condition," I say. "I wish to stay here another week. I need to prepare myself."

Richard treats me to another one of his long silences. Finally he says, "I have a request also. Of course you may stay here for another week, but I would ask that you allow me to visit you every day, and then escort you back to Bisham." He folds my hand into his. "It would be cruel to deny me the pleasure of your company."

What am I supposed to say to that?

BOOK II: ONE SEED SOWN

As long as I am alive, in truth,
no one will have the joy and pleasure of my love
except for this flower

FROM PLUS BELE QUE FLOR
MONTPELLIER CODEX, 13TH CENTURY

Chapter 1
Rouen Castle, Rouen, English France
Feast of Saint Anne, Mother of Our Lady
July 26, 1441

On a day when hot winds carried the sharp scent of herbs, I was riding back from a visit to the merchants of Rouen—one of several—when I heard the thunderous sound of hooves galloping toward me.

I stopped my palfrey on the slope that led up to the castle.

Was it Richard? He'd ridden out with his army to relieve Pontoise only two weeks ago, and I did not expect him so soon. I clutched at the reins, causing my gentle palfrey to snort and arch her neck.

Life as Richard's duchess was not as bad as I'd feared. I acquired a taste for gorgeous satin and thick velvet gowns of every hue, for fur robes, supple gloves, elegant boots, and jewelry. I grew to love the wink of precious gems, of emeralds, rubies, and sapphires, and in the summer months, I loved the subtle luster of pearls with lighter silks. Richard proved to be a considerate husband, sparing no expense to fit up his various residences for my pleasure. The only thing he would not tolerate was refusal when he wanted to bed me. He was gentle, but persistent.

And so I bore him three children in four years.

I hated the discomfort of pregnancy and the messiness and pain of birthing, but my children were lovely. My eldest, three-year-old Joan whom I named after Mama, was the apple of my eye. She was a charming child, already showing great beauty, and saying the funniest things. Her sister, two-year-old Nan, was a much quieter soul who glowed with contentment when playing with animals. Baby Henry, born in February, was only five months old and had yet to make his mark on the world. But Richard had been thrilled to have an heir.

Through the thin, semi-transparent fabric of my veil, I dimly saw a gentleman bring his white gelding to a stop with a flourish and vault off.

I pushed the material aside with my gloved hand.

Much younger than Richard, I guessed his age to be no more than twenty. He wore a tunic of dark green velvet over stockings that were half green, half gold with the seam straight up the middle of the front of each leg. The tunic was shorter than usual, and the eye-catching stockings drew attention to those legs, long and very shapely.

"Your Grace," he gasped in elegant French as he dropped to one knee in the dust. "You forgot this."

He handed up a package that contained my new dress, stiff with jewels.

I looked into a pair of laughing hazel eyes.

"Have I seen you before?"

"I was riding through Rouen when I saw your entourage. I'd heard much of your beauty, so I reined in to see if I could get a glimpse of such rare loveliness."

I turned my head to hide a faint blush. "How did you notice my package?"

"I saw it as soon as you left."

"How fortuitous that you should happen to be there at that precise moment."

His boots were coated in dust.

"Have you come from Pontoise?"

He nodded.

"Have you news of my lord?"

"Indeed I do, my lady. He is in good health and spirits and his campaign against the French is going well."

Richard and I had arrived in Rouen a month ago so that he could take up his post as governor of Normandy. The city of Rouen was the English capital of France, but the French had been trying for the past several years to wrest control of English France. Pontoise was an English town near Paris that controlled a strategic crossing over the River Oise. Whenever the French wanted to use this crossing, they were forced to pay English tolls, and this they did not like.

In early June, three weeks before our arrival, the French laid siege to Pontoise. But Richard appeared at the head of a large army, bringing his best generals. He was determined to teach the French a lesson. While the men fought the French, their wives and children kept me company.

At my asking, the young man went into detail about marches and counter-marches, night-crossings and chases back and forth across the River Oise. His brown hair bounced, as he gestured the army's movements with his hands, his lips equally mobile and expressive. He smelled of almonds, of nutmeg, and of some exotic spice I could not place. This was such a contrast to other men I knew, who smelled of dogs, horses, mud, and—other unmentionable things.

Who was he? Where did he live?

"Why don't you stay awhile and refresh yourself?"

I led the way into the great hall of Rouen Castle, summoned the servants, and saw that he was well furnished with refreshments. When I was assured that he had what he wanted, I left.

Around an hour or so later, I reappeared.

He was singing a chanson, accompanying himself on his lute. As soon as he saw me, he rose.

He devoured me with his eyes.

My new dress was of blue-grey silk with yards of material that floated around me as I walked. Pearls adorned the bodice. Pearls swirled in patterns down the sleeves. Pearls inscribed my name around the hem. I wore a matching heart-shaped headdress with a fine gauze veil.

It had been hard to decide which jewels to wear, for I had chests filled with them. It had taken Jenet a whole hour to find them all.

Eventually, I chose a sapphire and pearl necklace with matching earrings.

The silence lengthened as he gazed at me.

I lifted my chin and stared back. What would happen now? But our silent reverie was interrupted by the appearance of the other ladies. Word must have got around that an attractive stranger had arrived, for they wore their best dresses, coloring their cheeks and lips with rouge. After two weeks of nun-like seclusion while our men battled the French, we were dying for male company.

The young man got up and bowed, kissing each hand with a flourish.

I took in their finery and glanced down at my gown.

"You look ravishing, *duchesse*," murmured the young man. "You need no addition to your attire."

Richard's sister, now Isabel de Bourchier, married to Baron Henry Bourchier, bit her lip.

Lady Bess de Vere, married to John de Vere, twelfth Earl of Oxford, interrupted. "Do you know *Plus Bele Que Flor, The One To Whom I Submit Is More Beautiful Than A Flower?*"

"Now, how does that go, my lady?" said the young man as he sat and strummed some chords on his lute. "*The One To Whom I Prostrate Myself Is More Lovely Than A Flower?*"

Lady Margaret Beauchamp, Countess of Shrewsbury smiled. "*The One Who Lets Me Play For Her Is More Lovely Than A Flower.*"

"No," replied my sister-in-law Lady Lisette Beauchamp, married to George. "*The One Who Lies Beneath Me Is More Lovely Than A Flower.*"

I laughed. "No indeed. It is *The One Who Commands My Obedience Is More Lovely Than A Flower.*"

"You are looking very well, Cis," remarked Isabel in her distinctive voice. She lisped her *r*s exactly as Richard did. "That is quite a magnificent dress, I have never seen so many pearls. Who is that?"

Silence fell as I faced Isabel.

Lady Isabel de Bourchier was an unusually thin lady of thirty-two years. Of course, it would be Isabel asking the awkward questions, with her habit of watchful silence. "This young man, Isabel, has come from Pontoise."

Isabel turned towards him. "And you are?"

"My name is of no consequence, my lady." The young man rose and bowed gracefully.

Isabel's elegantly thin eyebrows rose. "Are you saying that you are of no consequence?"

There was silence.

"Where are you from?"

"A country far from here."

Isabel thinned her lips.

"Isabel," I said, touching her arm. "He has come from Pontoise. He has news of the campaign."

Immediately the ladies clamored for news about their husbands, all of them among Richard's generals: Isabel's husband, Baron Henry Bourchier, Bess's husband, the Earl of Oxford, and Lisette's husband, my brother George, Lord Latimer.

I held up my hand. "It's such a fine evening, with many more hours to run. Why don't we sit outside? We can discuss Pontoise."

I signaled to the servants to follow.

The young man put down his lute and offered me his arm.

I led everyone to an area out in the garden screened by yew, which made for a private kind of outside room. Inside this space were tubs of roses, rosemary, thyme, and small orange trees. A turf seat stood in the middle, looking as if three benches had been put into an oddly shaped triangle with a side left open. Sitting on the seat gave us a view out of this small garden through a doorway cut into the hedge. This view led the eye into the larger pleasure ground where a fountain fed the bathing pool.

I sat in the middle of the seat, with the young man on my right and Isabel on my left.

The others took the remaining places.

I turned to the young man, and he began his tale while the servants set up a table at the open side of the three-sided seat and brought cold beet soup, cheese, and manchet bread, followed by a salad and hare stew. This was followed by Hippocras and angel wafers.

"The French are playing a clever game," I remarked as I set my wine down. "By not coming out into the open to fight us fairly, they conserve their forces, while we wear ours out as we chase after them. Could we not employ a similar strategy to the French?"

The young man raised his brows. "You are quite right, my lady," he said. "What a strategist you are. I would not like to command an army that opposed yours."

I was about to reply when Bess said, "I'm thankful our men managed to cross the bridge of boats at Royaumont without breaking their necks. Our Blessed Lady be thanked for that." She dipped her head like a horse, chestnut curls bobbing.

"Men can be so reckless," agreed Margaret, wiping her fingers with a napkin. Her husband, the Earl of Shrewsbury, had been holding Pontoise for the English along with my brother William, Lord Fauconberg, before Richard's army arrived. Now they joined in his campaign against the French.

"We ladies have to be so strong," declared Lisette, stuffing another wafer in her mouth and licking the honey off her fingers. "Gentlemen have no idea how hard it is to wait and wait with no news." She batted her lashes at the young man. "Would you treat your wife like that?"

"I have no wife."

Lisette opened her small, raisin-like eyes wide. Small and plump, twenty-year-old Lisette was like a pigeon that constantly pecked at its feed. "You don't? A fine young man like yourself?"

"It's not so easy for someone with my kind of life."

"What kind of life? I've never met such a well-favored gentleman who hadn't been snatched—"

"Lisette means only that she is used to married couples," interrupted Margaret, flushing. "In our society, we are married at such a young age." Her voice trailed off.

"Before we know who we are," I said. "Before we even have the capacity to choose—so that we can't."

The young man shot me a sharp look. I twisted my napkin while Isabel picked up her horn-handled knife and peeled an orange.

"Have you heard the story of Black Fulk of Anjou?" she enquired, staring at the young man. She looked around. "Some of us here are descended from him. One day, he discovered his wife in the arms of her lover. Do you know what he did?"

The young man stared at her, unflinching.

"I will tell you," said Isabel, returning his stare. "He made his wife get into her wedding finery. Then he burned her alive in the town square at Angers."

There was silence for several moments, almost as if everyone was holding their breath. Then a sound made everyone turn.

It was Lisette. She slumped, white-faced into her seat.

Margaret got up. "She is not well," she said, frowning at Isabel, who daintily placed a piece of orange into her mouth. "I must take her back to her chamber."

I signaled to the steward, who bowed and put his hand under Lisette's elbow while Margaret stood on her other side. Between them, they propelled the limp figure back to the castle.

"She makes much out of nothing," said Isabel. "She creates these dramas."

"Your story was not pleasant," said Bess. She turned to me. "Is she easily upset?"

I hesitated. It was a delicate matter for Lisette, married to someone like my brother George, who had an unpredictable temper. Eventually I murmured, "She is not happy."

Isabel snorted. "Who is?"

I rose. "I fear I must bid you goodnight," I said to the young man. "Margaret might need my help."

The young man bowed. "Of course," he murmured, gazing at me as he kissed my hand.

I stepped into the shadows to hide my blushes while the others bade farewell to him.

"What a charming young man," declared Bess as we went back to the castle. "So well favored. Do you suppose we'll be seeing him again?"

"You can be sure of that," said Isabel. "He clearly enjoys gleaning information and gossip from wherever he can find it."

I didn't respond.

"I'll see you in the morning," said Bess, curtseying first to me, then to Isabel. She smiled at me as she stifled a yawn and disappeared up the stone staircase.

"You're quiet tonight, Cecylee," said Isabel, giving me a peck on the cheek.

"I am greatly fatigued, madam," I replied, sweeping her a low curtsey.

I spent that night waiting for dawn to break.

Chapter 2
Lammastide
August 1,1441

By Lammastide, the roses had reached their peak and clustered thickly up and over the arbor, providing not only shade but also a wonderful scent that intensified upon the evening.

It was my custom to sit in the arbor, by the bathing pool, with Margaret while we did our needlework. At thirty-seven years, Margaret was the eldest lady of my acquaintance, and during that long, hot summer, she became my dearest friend and confidante. Perhaps this was because Mama had so recently passed away.

How I missed Mama. Though we'd not seen much of each other these four years since my marriage to Richard, our messages brought me great comfort. Now she'd been gathered up to heaven, leaving a great hole in my life. Something Richard didn't understand.

I sighed. Why did *he* interest me so? I'd scarcely been able to keep him out of mind for the past week. "What do you want?" I murmured. Then, recollecting myself, I said to Margaret, "I wish I could give my lord another son. Little Henry is not strong. I fear he will not make old bones."

"Has he been coughing again?"

"Yes. He seems always to be sick with something, and it's high summer. What will happen when winter comes?"

Margaret leaned forward and patted my hand. "It is not in your hands, but in God's. Only God can tell whether your son will be spared."

"Is that so, Mama?" asked six-year-old Eleanor Talbot. Margaret's youngest was the most striking of her three daughters, with fair hair the color of silver and unusually colored eyes. Now, she tilted those violet eyes up to her mother's face.

"What about Our Blessed Lady?"

"Of course, she'd know as well," replied Margaret, smoothing back the child's silky hair.

"But wouldn't she know more than God?" asked Eleanor.

Margaret frowned. "I don't know, my sweet. Why do you think she would?"

Eleanor smiled, revealing even white teeth. "Because she's a lady, and ladies always know more than gentlemen."

"Why do you think that?" I asked. Where had the child got such ideas?

"Gentlemen do not always think with their heads," remarked Eleanor, executing a stem stitch.

"What do you mean child?" said Margaret. "Of course they do."

"Not always," replied Eleanor. "Sometimes they think with their pricks."

I flinched, the pleasant summer afternoon gone.

"Eleanor!" said Margaret, flushing. "Where did you hear that?"

Eleanor hung her head and fiddled with her work. "I was repeating only what Chantal said," she murmured. Chantal was a local girl who worked in the kitchens.

Margaret put a ringed finger under the child's chin, tilting it so that she could look directly into her daughter's eyes.

"That is not the sort of thing ladies say," she admonished gently. "You know your lord father wouldn't be pleased. And one day you'll be a married lady. You'll never be happy unless you learn to curb your tongue."

"Yes, Mama," murmured Eleanor, dimpling. "But suppose I wish to take the veil?"

Margaret was saved from replying by the appearance of a diminutive figure rushing over.

"Mama! Mama!"

Three-year-old Joan threw her arms around my neck. I smiled, taking her in. Joan's dark brown, almost black hair had come free from her headdress and was coiling down her back. She was dressed in a silken dress of dark blue that was stained and badly creased. Yet she looked carefree and happy.

Annette de Caux, both governess to the older children and nursemaid to baby Henry, followed Joan at a more sedate pace. She held Joan's discarded headdress in one hand. "Lady Joan," she exclaimed. "It is not seemly for you to wander with your hair so wild—" She broke off as she caught my eye and sank into a deep curtsey.

I smoothed Joan's loose hair and gathered her into my arms. I covered her soft cheeks with kisses.

Annette sighed and thinned her lips.

Joan tilted her head and smiled. "Mama," she said, clutching at my sleeve with sticky fingers. "Where've you been? I want to play ninepins."

"It's too hot to play now, my sweet," I murmured, brushing strands of hair out of Joan's face with the tips of my fingers. "And I'm busy. I must finish this sewing."

"But you're always busy nowadays," replied Joan, her lips quivering. "I only wanted to play for a little while." She pouted for a moment, then smiled.

I sighed. Joan was breathtakingly lovely, her eyes a deep blue, her face shaped like a heart. Pink roses bloomed in her cheeks. I held her more closely and inhaled her sweet scent.

"Why don't you let Annette take you to the kitchens?"

At this, Joan's face lit up. Annette folded her arms and shook her head.

"Are we going to be allowed to have sweetmeats?" Joan asked, running the tip of her tongue around her rosy lips.

Margaret laughed. "Yes indeed, you sweet child."

"Are you coming too, Margaret?" asked Joan as she scrambled off my lap.

"Lady Margaret," said Annette softly.

Margaret laughed again. "Your mother and I will come soon enough. We can play ninepins outside when it is cooler."

I bent and gave Joan one last kiss. "Go now," I said, giving her a gentle push.

"Come on, Eleanor," called Joan, holding out her hand to her friend. "We can go to the kitchens and eat as much as we like. Mama said."

Eleanor glanced at her mother, who nodded. She made her curtsey and waited for Joan.

Joan blew me a kiss and ran off with Eleanor.

Annette followed, chastising, "You should always remember to make your curtsey to your lady mother. You should always wear your headdress. Your lord father would be gravely displeased to see his eldest daughter behaving like a kitchen wench—" Her voice faded away as she continued to instruct three-year-old Joan on the proper way to behave.

Margaret and I looked at each other and burst into laughter. A sudden cloudburst prevented us from saying any more as we made for the castle swiftly.

An hour passed, the sun came out, and I was smoothing a tuck with my right ring finger on a dress I was making for Joan when I glanced up. My heart pulsed in my throat. Bess was with the young man in the gardens below. Their heads were close together as they strolled along.

"Look at that," declared Lisette. "She's got him all to herself. She never thinks about the rest of us."

"Lisette!" exclaimed Margaret, turning towards her youngest sister.

I pricked my finger. A spot of blood landed in the middle of the flower I'd been embroidering.

Margaret rose, took a basin of water, added salt, and with a linen cloth set about getting the bloodstain out of Joan's new dress.

The door opened and Bess danced in.

"Such a charming young man," she declared.

"No need to ask whom you've been with," remarked Isabel, snapping her ivory needlecase shut.

Bess turned to me. "The young man's name is Monsieur Pierre Blaybourne, and he's just joined the garrison here at Rouen as an archer."

"Now why would he do that?" asked Isabel.

Margaret looked at me closely as she continued to rub salt and cold water onto the bloodstain.

"He says he's doing it to protect Cecylee," replied Bess, laughing.

The room went very quiet as three pairs of eyes fell on me. Margaret's grey eyes grew thoughtful, Lisette's currant brown eyes flashed angrily, and Isabel's pale ones bore right through me.

I felt a shiver of a whiplash pass up my spine. I rose from my seat.

"I know nothing of this. I have not seen this...Blaybourne since the day we met a week ago."

Bess laughed and pulled at my sleeve. "There's no need to be so serious. He's invited all of us to the archery butts to see him practice with the other men. They are having a contest now and want us to judge who is the best archer."

Immediately, the solar hummed like a hive. Lisette jumped up and called for her maid to bring her new red dress. Margaret, Isabel, and I put our sewing away and summoned our women for rosewater and lavender water and for pastes made of angelica flowers and ground almonds to cleanse the skin.

Jenet helped take off my everyday blue linen and I slipped into a dusky rose silk worn over a pale green chemise. I studied my jewel case, deciding on pearls to go with the pink silk while Jenet tidied my hair and rearranged my headdress. By the time Jenet had finished dressing me, the other ladies were ready. Lisette was vivid in red, Bess's dress of the deepest green set off her green eyes and chestnut hair, Margaret wore heavy purple damask, and Isabel wore sky-blue silk.

The shower had cooled off the thundery weather. Outside, a light breeze lifted our veils, and we walked a well-trodden path amongst oak and hornbeam, beech, hazel and hawthorn, followed by servants bearing refreshments.

Just outside the city walls were the archery butts, small mounds of earth and stone used as platforms for practice targets. The targets themselves were limited only by the imagination. Sometimes the archers used scarecrows, sometimes a rough plank with crudely painted symbols. Today, they set up a well-dressed French soldier stuffed with straw. His tunic bore the royal arms of France.

A knot of perhaps twenty archers gathered a little distance away. They checked the horn knocks on their bows to be sure they held the string properly, waxed the bowstrings to ensure the arrows flew easily, and wound silk thread through the flights of each arrow to hold the goose feather quills firmly to the arrow shaft. As we approached, Blaybourne separated from the crowd, smiling and bowing. He was attired in a brown linen tunic and hose, topped with a leather jerkin, an outfit that blended in perfectly with the other men on the Rouen garrison.

"I am charmed that such lovely ladies should grace our archery contest—".

"Who wins?" Bess asked, fixing her green eyes on him. "Is it the person who shoots the fastest?"

"Or perhaps the one who is most accurate?" asked Margaret.

"Or perhaps the tallest and most well-favored gentleman?" put in Lisette smiling up at him.

"And what think you, my lady?" asked Blaybourne, turning towards me.

"Shooting accurately and quickly are important, of course," I replied, "but perhaps we should also look at how well kept each archer's kit is, because that gives some indication of his character."

He bowed.

"Or perhaps," I put in laughing, as a sudden thought struck me, "it should be how *untidy* it is."

He raised an eyebrow.

"Yes," I said. "How untidy it is, on the grounds that an archer who can shoot both fast and accurately and yet has the most untidy tackle, must have a very quick and agile mind in order to be able to find what he needs in the midst of such shambles."

He clapped his hands and laughed. "An unusual contest. So let me see, the other ladies will judge speed and accuracy."

I smiled.

"And you, my lady, will judge for yourself how untidy he is."

Everyone murmured assent, and we arranged ourselves on the benches under the oak tree like brightly colored birds. The marshal held up his hand, then let it fall. The archers nocked and drew. They aimed, then let fly with hand following string almost as swiftly as the arrows flew. Bow strings twanged, arrows whistled, as the archers reached for the next arrow in belt or quiver, to nock and draw, aim and let fly, in a lethal, unrelenting hail of arrows.

Two archers lined up at a time to shoot, standing sideways to the direction of the target and drawing to ear or jaw. By this method of doublets—which I had suggested— we eventually narrowed the contestants down to Blaybourne and his rival, also tall and barrel-chested, but dark, scowling, and rough in his manners.

Both stood there: the scowling churl frowning as he nocked and drew with his right hand, while Blaybourne faced him, wearing gloves of soft tanned leather, using his left hand to knock and draw. Both arrows flew, but the one from Blaybourne pierced the heart of the stuffed French soldier, who toppled over into a heap of straw and old clothes. There was a cheer, followed by laughter as Blaybourne came back to receive our congratulations.

Even Isabel was quite warm in her praise.

"I've not seen a left-handed archer before," she remarked. "Can you shoot with your right hand too?"

"I'm sure he can," put in Lisette, her usually pasty complexion tinged with pink. She drained her cup of wine. "He could pierce anybody's heart with either hand," she giggled.

Isabel looked at her, but Lisette drained another cup of wine.

"My lady Cecylee, would you like to inspect the archers?" inquired Blaybourne with a bow.

Smiling, I took his arm. "It has to be suitably untidy," I remarked, tilting my head. "Somewhat untidy will not be good enough."

"And what does my lady consider to be suitably untidy?" he asked laughing.

I felt a flutter in my chest, so I frowned.

"You take this very seriously."

"Indeed I do. I do not give my favors away lightly."

Blaybourne raised his eyebrows but did not reply.

Each archer laid out his things on a piece of rough cloth. There was the bow, which was about five and a half feet long. There was the bow case, made of canvas. There was the leather quiver to hold the arrows, the arrows with their goose-feather quills, leather belts to tie the quiver around the waist, arm guards or bracers, and finger tabs to protect the fingers from the bowstring. There was also wax, silken thread, horn nocks and various tools for repair.

At length, I came upon one that was very untidy. As I straightened up, my eyes met Blaybourne's.

"Yours?" I queried.

He smiled.

"You knew—"

"I did not. I left it here just as you see."

I shook my head.

"It is true," he said, "I am naturally untidy. I am always losing things."

Another archer standing nearby agreed. "Yes, my lady. Untidy, that's what he is."

Soon there was a chorus of nodding men.

"How unfortunate," I murmured, "for that means you win."

"How can that be unfortunate?"

"It will make you unpopular," I remarked, looking at the other archers who were staring at me expectantly.

I raised my voice. "I am awarding two prizes. The first is the duke's prize for the fastest and most accurate archer, who has the tidiest kit."

I beckoned to the scowling man who came forward, his face now wreathed in smiles, as I gave him a badge made in the likeness of Richard's white lion. He pinned it onto his tunic with a flourish.

"Next, I present the duchess's prize for the fastest and most accurate archer who has the untidiest kit."

I pinned another emblem onto Blaybourne's tunic. It showed a rose tree with a castle in the background. "It signifies the Rose of Raby, which is what folk called me when I was a girl," I murmured.

"I will treasure this with my life." He took my hand and kissed each finger separately.

My cheeks burned, for it reminded me of a gesture Richard had made when he'd come courting. Why was I being so foolish? My embarrassment was sure to set tongues wagging.

Blaybourne nodded to the marshal, who came beside him and whispered something. The marshal signaled to the men from the garrison, and they departed in the direction of the castle. Then Blaybourne turned to the others watching. "Which of you ladies would like to try your hand at archery?"

Isabel went first, but she needed no instruction.

"How deft she is," remarked Margaret. "I'd no idea she was so talented."

Then he bowed and asked Margaret to try.

"I don't know if I should at my age."

"My lady, you are not old," he said, "and it will do you good."

He handed her his gloves and tied a leather arm guard on each arm.

Margaret drew. The arrow hit the ground in front of her with a thud.

"Try to look up, my lady. And pull to your ear."

This time the arrow whistled off and landed several yards away.

The ladies clapped, but Margaret, breathing heavily, handed the bow and gloves back to the archer.

"I do not wish to tempt fate," she said smiling. "Let the others try."

Lisette went next. Turning her head sideways, she gazed up at him through her lashes while he gave instructions.

"Lisette," murmured Margaret.

The arrow flew but landed only a yard or so away.

"Oh dear," remarked Lisette. "I don't feel very stable. Perhaps if you were to steady my arm?"

She gazed at him and crumpled to the ground.

I took a linen napkin from a servant to wipe her face, which was now beaded in sweat.

Margaret knelt beside her and gently unlaced her red gown.

Bess laid a hand on her cheek. "She seems feverish. We should take her inside."

Lisette opened her eyes. "I don't wish to go."

"You're not well," said Margaret.

"I shall take her back to the castle," said Isabel.

She signaled to the servants, who helped Lisette to her feet and divested her of the gloves, arm-guards and bow he had given her. They placed her in a litter and took her back to the castle.

Margaret and Isabel followed.

I remained with Bess and Blaybourne, looking at the retreating figures, when Bess said, "I have always wanted to try my hand at archery. May I?"

"Of course, my lady," he said. He tied the leather arm-guards on, handed her his gloves, and gave her his bow.

I felt suddenly weary, so I sat down under the oak tree and closed my eyes.

I must have gone out for a moment, for I came to with a start when he called out, "Perfect, my lady. You will be a fine archeress one day."

"With such an excellent teacher, how could I help that?" Bess replied laughing.

He was silent.

I rose and signaled to the servants to offer them some refreshments.

"I wondered where you were, my lady, I thought perhaps you'd gone," he said.

"I was seeing about the refreshments. Would you like something? Bess? It is a hot afternoon, and shooting arrows must be tiring work."

"No thank you," said Bess as she gave the gloves, arm-guards, and bow back to him. "I will go and see if Margaret needs my help."

She disappeared in the direction of the castle.

"Do we need the servants here, my lady?"

I looked at him for a long moment. I knew I shouldn't be alone with him, but—

"Perhaps not," I murmured and beckoned to the steward.

Soon the servants were disappearing down the path to the castle. A breeze stirred and a bird trilled an arpeggio. We were completely alone.

He touched my arm. "And now it is your turn, Cecylee."

My head jerked up.

Our gaze held. Then he handed me the bow and the finger-tabs and tied the arm-guards on.

I lifted the bow, drew the string back, and aimed. But my first shot fell in front of my feet.

He came closer and, standing just behind me, put his hands on mine. His hands burned into my skin, yet gave me strength.

"It's like this," he murmured softly. "You look up, not down, you draw back as far as you can, and then—"

"You take the consequences?"

"Exactly," he said, as I fired off a shot that landed several yards away, right in the middle of the painted board that had been chosen as the target.

"That was excellent, Cecylee."

He was so close that I could inhale the spicy scent and feel his body just touching my back. Now, I felt his breath on my cheek. One step more, and he cradled me in his arms. Ignoring my pounding heart, I fired off another shot.

It landed in the ground several yards away.

"Should we continue?" he murmured, brushing my cheek with a butterfly kiss.

I gave him the bow.

"I must stop now."

He kissed my cheek again and squeezed me gently.

"You're not angry with me?"

"No. But this is unwise."

"Indeed it is. But I've longed for this moment, ever since I first saw you."

His eyes were like a clear pool that refreshed my soul. "I feel so drawn to you," he said. "I tried to keep away but I could not."

"You make me feel as if I've come home," I replied.

Our lips met in a kiss.

I melted. Then I pulled back.

"I must go." I took off the finger tabs and arm-guards, handed them to him, and turned.

He put a hand on my arm.

I gazed into his eyes, my cheeks warming.

"I must go."

I turned on my heel and forced myself to walk away, feeling his gaze scorching into my back with every step that I took.

Chapter 3
Feast of Saint Clare
August 12, 1441

Lisette's illness continued, and after ten days, we needed more medicine.

I could have sent a servant to the Abbey of Saint-Ouen, but I was longing for fresh air. I should have gone with an escort, for Richard had enjoined me never to ride abroad without protection. But I was tired of being surrounded by various people. Bess agreed to accompany me, and so, leaving Lisette in the care of Margaret and Isabel, we set off early one morning just after dawn while it was cool.

As we came into the courtyard where our horses waited, a tall figure detached itself from the shadows and came forward. Bess gasped and clutched at my arm, but as soon as the light fell on the figure she relaxed into a smile.

"Ladies," Blaybourne called, bowing low. "What brings you out so early?"

"Lisette is not well," replied Bess going up to him. "She continues feverish, and we are riding off to the Abbey of Saint-Ouen to get fresh medicines."

"Allow me to escort you," said Blaybourne. He looked at me.

I opened my mouth to decline, but Bess assented.

Blaybourne helped us onto our horses, vaulted onto his white gelding, and we set off.

It was a glorious morning, the air was fresh and cool, the meadows a riot of flowers, with blue cornflowers, pink heather, and yellow meadow-rue. The trees were thickly leaved, and their leaves rustled as we rode past. I held back so that I rode behind Blaybourne and Bess. They spent the entire journey riding side by side, chattering amiably.

I remained silent. I spent ten days devoting myself to Lisette, amusing the children, and playing the gracious hostess to the merchants and aristocrats passing through Rouen, wanting to visit with the governor of Normandy's wife. I expended an enormous effort on keeping my mind off the one thing that kept powerfully drawing me towards it, like a lodestone: my feelings for Blaybourne.

Blaybourne meant many things to me. For one, he was a pleasure to look at. Now he sat gracefully on his gelding, using subtle motions of his long fingers to guide it. Everything he did had a kind of ease and charm, so different from Richard. Richard rarely vaulted onto his horse, for he was becoming stout and often needed his groom to help him up.

Then he was so well tuned to me, he seemed able to read my thoughts before I was aware of having them. I remembered his kindness and sensitivity at the archery tournament, when my fiery blushes had given me away. Every time we talked, our interactions were like a duet, alternating effortlessly with perfect timing, without one having to wait for the other to catch up. With Richard, I had always to remember to be patient, for he ran at a slower speed.

Most alarming of all, I felt the stirrings of something I didn't even know I could feel. It made my affection for Richard seem pallid by comparison. I didn't understand it. How could I feel so passionate about someone I scarcely knew?

And there he was, riding a few feet in front of me, being courteously gallant to Bess. Yet Bess did not seem to be making much progress. She was trying hard enough, telling amusing stories, and little morsels of gossip, but Blaybourne seemed distracted, sometimes asking her to repeat things, sometimes not getting her jests.

I sighed. How was I going to make him go away? And what had he been doing in the courtyard at that hour? Had he been waiting for someone? Had he been waiting for *me*? At that thought, my heart leapt in my throat and started thudding. What was wrong? I never felt this disquieted. I was noted for being serene, yet every time I thought about Blaybourne, my heart interrupted.

I was in such a brown study I didn't notice how far we'd come until Bess pulled on my bridle.

"Cecylee!" she exclaimed. "We're here. Do you not see that?"

I pulled myself out of my thoughts with an effort and attempted to smile, although I felt more like weeping.

Blaybourne walked up to me, frowning. "You look pale, my lady. Perhaps you should sit under this horse chestnut. It provides a goodly shade, and I will get you some refreshment."

This was the last thing I wanted, but conflicting thoughts and feelings left me dumbstruck. I looked at Bess in silent appeal, sure that she wouldn't want to leave me alone with the attractive young man she'd been cultivating for the last half-hour.

But Bess jumped down and said, "I'll get the medicines then." And blowing me a kiss, she disappeared.

I set my mouth grimly as Blaybourne helped me down, willing myself not to notice how it felt to be in his arms. I wandered over to the bench and sat down, examining the patch of dusty ground beneath my feet, each blade of grass, the marks on my boots, the white dust dredging the hem of my gown. At length, Blaybourne returned bearing a tray of cider with pastries warm from the oven. The aroma of those pastries was so seductive, I could not help looking up.

It was a mistake.

Blaybourne's eyes were warm, soft, and deep. His mouth curved into a tender smile.

My heart resumed its hammering.

"I don't know what's wrong with me. I don't feel well. I should've let Bess come by herself."

"But then I would have missed seeing you," he remarked, as he set the tray down and handed me a cup of cider. "Or is that what you are trying to say?"

"Just what were you doing in the castle courtyard at that hour?"

"Waiting for you. What else could I possibly have been doing?"

"You could have been doing any of a number of things." I lowered my lashes and sipped my cider. Finally, I looked into his face.

His eyes were warm, and his mouth curved into its gentle smile.

I smiled back.

He leaned over and kissed me on the lips, a long, luxurious, and increasingly passionate kiss. "My sweet," he murmured. "You know very well I can't keep away from you. I've been waiting for more than a week for you to appear."

"What about Bess?"

He caressed my cheek with a long finger. The sensation made me tingle all over. "No, the question is, do I mean anything to you?"

"You mean the whole world to me. I've been miserable without you."

He held me close, brushing my hair and cheeks with his lips. "Would you meet me in the garden this evening, around compline? It'll be quieter then, and we can spend some precious moments together."

"I'll be there," I promised as he kissed every finger of my hand, front and back.

"I'm the happiest man in the world," he murmured, and then Bess appeared.

Blaybourne rose to help her with her packages. As before, I hung back so Blaybourne and Bess again rode side-by-side, chatting. I had a strange feeling in the pit of my stomach, as if a large piece of lead had lodged itself there. I could hardly believe I was taking such a risk. And what of Blaybourne and the risk he was taking? He was a good archer, but could he fight with a sword? Richard was an excellent swordsman—

My mind veered off into these depths as I attempted to keep my horse from wandering off the track.

Eventually we reached the castle, and Blaybourne helped Bess down and summoned a servant to look after her packages.

Then he came for me.

He slowly led my horse into a secluded nook between the stables and the gardens, and gently he carried me in his arms as he lifted me down off my horse. We lingered.

Reluctantly, I pulled away. "I must go." I gave him one final kiss.

"I'll be in the garden, my love, at compline."

"By the fountain?"

"By the fountain." And clasping his hand one last time, I flew across the courtyard and up the stairs, tearing myself away from him.

As I entered my chamber, Jenet rose and curtseyed. She was now around thirty, but looked as slender as she had at fourteen. Her black eyes grazed me, intense and direct.

"My lady, whatever has happened?"

I blushed.

"An attractive young man?"

"Really, Jenet! What has happened to you? You used to be as quiet as a mouse."

Jenet busied herself in unpinning my veil and removing my headdress.

"I beg your pardon, my lady. I didn't mean to be rude. It's just that I've never seen you look so radiant."

"You never used to be so lively and so free with your opinions when Audrey was around."

"If you remember, my lady, Audrey loved to talk. It was difficult to get a word in edgewise." She brushed my hair. "I miss my aunt and your lady mother. It is hard to believe they are no longer here."

After Mama died nine months ago at her manor of Howden-le-Wear, near Castle Raby, Audrey was soon dead herself.

"Audrey was devoted to Mama," I said slowly, stumbling through thoughts as Jenet's fingers worked at my hair. "She was her best friend and confidante. She nursed her through all her pregnancies and comforted her when Alainor was snatched away as a child-bride. I remember Mama saying once that she didn't know what she would've done without Audrey."

"And your lady mother was so kind to my aunt," said Jenet. "She allowed her to stay on, even though she had a child out of wedlock. She saw to it that he was trained as a cook, so that he could work in the castle kitchens."

An image of Perrequin's elaborate sugar sculptures filled my head. He'd made two of them the day of my betrothal.

There was a pause while Jenet braided my hair into plaits and fashioned them into an elaborate hairdo.

"What did the young gentleman say?"

"It has nothing to do with you."

"Indeed it does, my lady." She paused to look into my face.

I lowered my lashes and set my mouth into a line.

Jenet sighed. "He didn't make any suggestions—"

My lashes flew up as my cheeks warmed.

Jenet's mouth opened.

I turned away and studied my jewels.

"My lady, I know I am bold for saying this, but you plunge headlong into things—"

"Have you ever been in love?"

"My lady—"

"I am powerless—"

"But you're not, my lady. Don't go to him. He doesn't have anything to lose. You do."

I glared.

"I heard a story this very morning," said Jenet. "I was breaking my fast in the kitchens when a traveler told me a story about an Italian count who murdered his lady wife after he found her in bed with a lover. Chopped off her head, he did—"

"My lord would never do something like that!"

"Of course not, my lady," said Jenet, gently turning my head so that she could continue making the hairdo. "I never meant to suggest so. But—"

"We will talk no more of this," I said.

And I kept silence while Jenet finished dressing my hair, washed my face and hands in rosewater, and arrayed me in a richly embroidered green silk dress.

During the rest of that long, hot day, I kept to my seat in the solar next to Isabel as I sewed the children's clothes. My needle flew with an eerie energy as I embroidered flowers, made buttonholes, and ran up hems and seams.

The time for compline came and went.

I heard laughter coming from the garden below, and looking down, saw Lisette with Blaybourne. I blinked. I hadn't known Lisette was well enough to get up. When Margaret flew to her side, trying to convince her to return to her room, I understood.

Lisette put her hand on Blaybourne's sleeve. "It's such a lovely evening, will you not walk?"

I did not hear his reply, but Lisette threw her head back, laughter bubbling up from her throat. Blowing him a kiss, she was escorted back into the castle by Margaret.

Without thinking, I got up and craned my head through the window.

Blaybourne raised his hand and beckoned.

I clutched at the heavy draperies.

"Is something wrong, Cecylee?" said Isabel. "You mustn't let silly little Lisette get on your nerves. She's not worth your time."

I resumed my seat. "You are quite right," I murmured when the door flew open and Lisette came in, supported by Margaret.

"He's taking me to the abbey tomorrow. He said it would do me good to ride out and get fresh air."

Isabel turned to stare at her. "Your husband is fighting in Pontoise. Who could you possibly be talking of?"

Lisette flung herself down.

"I feel much better. I agree with our charming friend, fresh air will make me feel well again, especially as he'll have to help me on and off my horse. How it will feel to be in his arms—" She closed her eyes and smiled dreamily.

I dropped any pretense of sewing and looked at Margaret. "Is she well?"

"Obviously not," snapped Isabel. She rose. "I will not have it said that we ladies are so uncontrollable we fly towards the first pot of honey we see while our husbands risk their lives in battle."

Lisette rose, hectic spots of red flaring on her cheeks. "I'm going out with him tomorrow."

Isabel turned to Margaret. "I strongly suggest we give her a draught of poppy juice to calm her down."

"I'm not a child!" Lisette stamped her foot, then swooned.

Isabel nodded to Margaret, and between them, they bundled up the limp figure and carried her off to bed.

I sat there, stunned. Were they going to drug Lisette? What had Blaybourne said to her? I closed my eyes and imagined Lisette in Blaybourne's arms. I could feel his breath, hear her giggles, imagine what might happen.

But why should I care? What was he against Richard and four years of marriage? I knew scarcely anything about him—not of his family, where he came from, what his station in life was, or what he was doing in Rouen.

What was he doing in Rouen?

There was a soft footfall, and someone entered the room. My eyes flew open. And there he was.

I rose slowly; the room swirled.

With catlike grace, Blaybourne caught me in his arms.

"You shouldn't be here."

"Come, my love."

"I shouldn't."

"I adore you," he said, kissing my cheek.

At that moment, the door to Lisette's chamber opened a crack. But no one came out.

He grabbed my hand, and we ran down the stairs into the courtyard, through the garden, until we came to the private screened-in area.

I turned away to compose myself, for I was short of breath, and the pins in my hair were coming loose.

"My love, do you remember you promised to meet me at compline?"

I put the last tendrils of hair back into place. "I am the governor of Normandy's wife."

"Has someone upset you?"

"Another story of a jealous husband. This time he beheaded his lady wife."

"Who told you that?"

"Does it matter?"

He was silent.

"What about you? Can you fight with a sword? My husband is extremely skilled with his."

"I have ways of protecting myself."

"Do you?"

He flushed. "I am sorry to have troubled you, madam."

He turned and walked slowly away.

I stood there, watching him go, wrapping my arms around me. My fingers were cold, my hands were cold, my arms were cold. I moved towards him. "Don't go!"

Blaybourne turned and raised an eyebrow.

I went to him.

He folded his arms around me. "You are sure?"

I nestled against him and nodded.

He covered my mouth with kisses and stroked me with long, nimble fingers, sweeping me away in a wave that was so fierce, I could no longer fight.

I unwound myself, kissed him on the forehead, and sighed.

Alert in an instant, Blaybourne dressed with deft motions, then helped me into my chemise.

I leaned against him, my hair hanging loose to my waist. "I've broken my marriage vows."

Our eyes locked. "Did you choose your husband?"

"You know there is no choice."

"And if there were?" he asked, stroking my hair. "Would you have me?"

I wrapped my fingers around his. "If I were free. But I'm trapped inside my marriage."

"I could protect you."

"But you're just an archer."

"Do you think so?"

I sneezed.

He put my gown on over my chemise and tied the laces. He was in the middle of helping me with my hair when we heard footsteps. We gave each other a quick glance, then Blaybourne melted into the shadows.

I rose to my feet, fumbling for my shoes.

"Cecylee!"

The cold voice cut through the warm air like a knife.

I drew myself up, but couldn't think of anything to say. Isabel's cold blue eyes raked me from head to toe, and from toe to head.

My cheeks burned.

"Have you thought of what it would do to Richard if he found out?" she asked, biting off each word in cold fury. I stared at the ground, a whiplash of fear prickling up my spine. "I'm surprised at you, Cecylee, I thought you had more sense."

I twisted my hands.

"I have been so stupid. Here I have been protecting your brother George's honor, trying to get his flighty Lisette to behave, when I should have been protecting Richard's honor."

I hung my head.

"Do you not care about Richard?"

"Richard is not Black Fulk—"

"You don't need to tell *me* that!" snapped Isabel. "He isn't going to burn his wife in her wedding finery, however badly she behaves."

"But—"

Isabel jerked my chin up. "Look at me. Remember your heroine Queen Alainor? Do you know what her husband did to her when she betrayed him? He locked her up for sixteen years."

"Queen Alainor outlived her husband."

"Is that all you can think of, outliving Richard?"

I squirmed. "Queen Alainor lived for another fifteen years and helped her sons rule England."

"You snake in the grass," hissed Isabel, sounding like a snake herself. "You care nothing for the House of York."

"Enough," said Blaybourne, quietly but firmly, materializing out of the shadows.

"How dare you," said Isabel. She turned towards me. "How could you lower yourself with an archer on the Rouen garrison?"

"You don't know anything about me."

As Isabel stared at him, my mind sluggishly went to work, like a millwheel churning up muddy water.

"You have grievously injured my brother."

He was silent.

Isabel leaned forward. "Do you deny it?"

"Did Cecylee choose her husband?"

"What does that have to do with anything?"

"Did you choose your husband?"

Isabel stared at him.

"I understand you had two husbands. Your first marriage to Sir Thomas Grey was annulled, was it not?"

Isabel tightened her jaw.

I scrutinized his face. How did he know that? That happened over fifteen years ago.

"I believe on the grounds of cruelty?"

She was silent.

"Your husband beat you, didn't he?"

I recoiled. An image sprang to mind of Isabel as a young woman visiting Castle Raby on the occasion of my betrothal to Richard. She was pale and thin and complained of pains in the stomach. When I asked Mama about it, she told me it was women's troubles. Now, I wondered. It explained a lot: the watchfulness, the sourness, the pleasure she took in unpleasant tales.

"How dare you cross-question me like this," said Isabel, her voice rasping. "I am a great lady. I am above such things. Yet here you are, digging for dirt—" She went into a spasm of coughing.

He ignored her. "That marriage was not of your choosing, was it? You were only four years old when you were married to him."

I winced. That was bad as anything that had happened to Alainor.

"I do not choose to discuss this with a stranger!"

"As you wish. But remember that you had a terrifying experience with a husband foisted on you when you were a small child. Why can't you be more compassionate to Cecylee?"

"Because my brother is no monster!"

"Isabel," I put in. "I do not expect you to understand —"

"Understand? I do not understand why Richard loves you."

"That marriage was not of my choice."

"Choice! What makes you think you would choose well for a husband?"

"I have a right to choose."

"You should be thinking of the family honor."

"My happiness is at stake."

"Is *he* well chosen?"

I folded my hand into Blaybourne's.

"Your behavior has been disgraceful."

"I want to be happy in my life."

"You have grievously injured the House of York, and if I had any say over the matter, you would be severely punished!"

Isabel glared at me. Then she swept off in the direction of the castle.

Chapter 4
Feast of Bernard of Clairvaux
August 20, 1441

I did not leave the castle until one evening a week
later. The day had been especially warm, Lisette had just
recovered, and to celebrate we went out to the bathing pool
to cool ourselves with a bathe in the evening air. We lingered,
gossiping and playing with the children, but at length
everyone went in, leaving me gazing at the brightening stars.
The night was peaceful and I ached for some of its quietude
before I had to go back into that hot, noisy, and smelly castle.

I lay back in the pool, half closing my eyes to let the
sounds of the evening wash over me. I was unaware of
anything other than the turmoil of my thoughts, unleashed
against the quiet backdrop of the night.

"My sweetest flower, how sad you look."

I started. "What are you doing here?"

"I must talk to you," he said in a low tone.

I stared. Where had he come from?

"You could be carrying my child."

"No."

"I will wait while you dress yourself." He disappeared
into the shadows.

I clambered out of the pool, grabbed my chemise and
threw it over my head, followed by my silk gown, which had
become water-stained and ruined by my splashes. Sighing, I
sat on the bench, finger-combing my hair and making a half-
hearted attempt to braid it, when he returned.

"Who are you?"

"Truly I don't want to talk about myself." He pulled
me gently to him and kissed me slowly and luxuriously on the
lips.

"You are not answering the question."

"Could it not wait?"

"I have been thinking, since last we met. I realize I
have agreed to marry someone whom I know not. Isabel is

right to chastise me. How can I make such a choice about one whom I know nothing?"

There was a pause.

"Let us start with your name. Is it really *Blaybourne*?"

He turned away from me and gazed into the bathing pool for a long moment. A breeze stirred faint ripples. I put my hand on his shoulder.

"You may not like what I have to say, for my family is humble. My father was a blacksmith in the village of Blay, near Bayeux in Normandy."

The color drained from my cheeks. I was silent for several long moments. "But you do not have the manners of a blacksmith," I stuttered.

"I was sent to the *Abbaye-aux-Hommes* in Caen as soon as I turned seven, for my parents were dead, my elder brother had a family to support, and there was no money for my keep."

I stood silent for a long time, trying to imagine this. "Is it usual for poor children to be sent away to the monastery?"

"If they are lucky. Otherwise they have to beg at the side of the road."

I shuddered. I had seen such children of course, many times, but had never given thought as to what their lives were like.

"I did well at the abbey, so when I turned twelve they sent me to study languages at the *Abbaye de Saint-Maurice* on Lake Geneva. I studied Italian and German as well as French, Latin, and Greek."

There he stood, now gazing into the pool. The son of a blacksmith. I had allowed myself to be touched by a peasant. My cheeks burned with shame. But his manners were excellent, highly polished and courtly. His voice was musical and cultivated. He dressed well. He was clean.

"I know you feel betrayed," he said, flushing and twisting the ring on his finger. It was a sapphire set in silver. His fingers were long, thin, and aristocratic-looking. They did not bear the marks of hard labor.

"You have not led the life of a peasant."

"No. But I started out that way."

"But you have made something of yourself. You were not born with riches as I was. You had to work to make your way in the world."

He gazed at me. "That is a rather unusual thing for a great lady to say."

I put my hands into his. "I've never felt this way about anyone before."

His lips met mine, and we lingered together for a long moment. "Beloved," he whispered, "I hardly dared hope—"

I stopped his mouth with my fingers. "I want to know more."

"I spent a couple of years at the *Abbaye de Saint-Maurice*. Then I was sent to university, in Italy."

"Where?"

He smiled and shook his head slightly.

"Are you a bachelor?"

"I'm a doctor."

I stared. I'd never met anyone so well educated. The aristocratic men I knew lived and died in the saddle. A vision of myself with this gentleman filled my head. We would study together, have soaring conversations.

"How did you become an archer?"

"I learned various trades."

"Is your name Blaybourne?"

"My name is Pierre de Blay, from the village in Normandy where I was born."

"Where does 'bourne' come from?"

He was silent.

I frowned. "Bourne" was an old English name for stream, like the north-country "burn." Many villages had "bourne" in their name, like Pangbourne, Fishbourne, Nutbourne. "Are you going to tell me anything else?"

"Not now."

"But—"

"All in good time, my sweet. You need to think about what I've said, and if you remember, I wanted to speak with you."

I nestled against him like a bird that has found her home. Suddenly I didn't care where he'd come from, only what he meant to me now.

He held me close. "Would he lock you up?"

"Is that why you wanted to see me?"

He nodded. "Would he harm you?"

I froze. Richard loved me, and yet—

"I would have to hide you somewhere."

"But I am the Duchess of York."

"Today is the twentieth day of August. I will return on the morning of the twenty-third to await your answer. I will meet you in the great hall of the castle where you hold your public audiences."

"But that's too dangerous."

"It will not be dangerous, I assure you."

"But how?"

"You will see, my sweet. Be sure to wear your pearl dress that day." He kissed my hand, bowed, and vanished.

Next day, I took to my bed. "Whatever shall I do when Richard returns?" I asked Margaret, when she came to visit me with Bess.

"Perhaps he'll not know."

Bess kissed my cheek.

"Are you not angry?" I asked.

"Why?"

"You liked him well."

"Indeed I did," replied Bess.

"Why did you leave me alone with him at the abbey?"

She patted my hand and smiled. "I have never seen two people so in love as the two of you. I knew you could not have long with your husband returning. I thought such lovers deserved to have some precious moments together."

Annette entering my chamber woke me. She carried Joan, who sobbed hard.

I cuddled her on my lap. "Whatever is the matter?"

"Madam, I know not," replied Annette. "Lady Joan seemed in good spirits this forenoon. I put her down for a nap, as I usually do. But she awoke screaming. I can do nothing with her."

I turned to the limp figure in my lap, gently cupping my hands around her little face. "What is it, sweetheart?"

"Mama, Mama," sobbed Joan, her tears making a wet patch on my silken chemise.

I stroked her hair and rubbed her back. "Come now, my dearest child. Tell me what troubles you so. Mama is here. You are safe. Whatever is wrong?"

Joan lifted a tear-stained face. "Don't leave!" She buried her face in my gown and sobbed.

I stiffened. "What is this?"

"I know not, madam," said Annette, going pale.

"Has she talked of this before?"

"No, madam, I don't think so."

"Who has been talking?"

"I would not like to say—"

"Come now," said Margaret, getting up from her place on the window seat. "Remember, your loyalty is to Duchess Cecylee. If someone has upset Lady Joan, she needs to know who."

Annette blanched. "Lady Lisette," she whispered. "She said she would curse me if I told anyone. She told me she would put a spell on me so that I would wither away before my time."

"That's nonsense," exclaimed Margaret. "Lisette should not be saying such wicked things. I'll find her at once and bring her here."

Margaret returned not only with Lisette, but with all the women. Jenet was there, and Margaret's woman, Bess's woman, Lisette's woman, and even Isabel's woman. Keeping

Joan on my lap, I faced them all. "For the sake of my children and for peace in my family, I ask you not to gossip."

Lisette smiled.

I handed Joan, now quiet, to Annette and rose. "Was it you?"

Lisette remained silent.

"I find my daughter sobbing her heart out, my maid frightened out of her life—"

"That's nothing to what you did. You broke your marriage vows. You sinned against your husband."

I slapped her across the cheek. "You will say no more. Do you understand?"

Lisette faced me, holding her hand to her cheek. Her eyes flashed. "Why should I help you? You always get what you want."

Margaret interrupted. "If you don't promise," she replied, her gentle grey eyes turned to steel, "I could go to George and hint that his wife's behavior was not what he would have wished."

Lisette jutted out her chin.

"You threw yourself at him every opportunity you got," said Bess.

"He didn't want *you*," said Lisette, rounding on her.

The room fell silent.

Lisette looked from one to the other, her face flushed, her under lip jutting out. At last, she turned to me and made the sign of the Horned King.

"I curse you, Cecylee! May you have a long and unhappy life!"

I fell into a chair. "You couldn't mean that."

But Lisette had gone.

Chapter 5
Saint Bartholomew's Eve
August 23, 1441

It was a bright hot morning. I sat on the dais in the great hall of the castle of Rouen, struggling to listen carefully to a stream of petitioners. The steward from Fotheringhay Castle in Northamptonshire wanted to pursue a land dispute. There were several merchants from Rouen wanting to show off their wares. There were people from Normandy seeking redress from the governor's wife over land, marriage settlements gone awry, and taxes.

I shifted in my seat. I should have sent a message to Blaybourne, telling him not to come. But I had somehow forgotten to do so. I drew a handkerchief from my sleeve and dried my moist palms.

A fanfare of trumpets sounded, and a page appeared, a boy of around nine or so, attired in a white satin tunic and hose. He wore white shoes and had a white hat on his head. He approached the dais bearing a ring on a white velvet cushion.

"My master wishes, madam, to present you with this ring."

As he knelt, I moved forward to accept the present. The ring was magnificent. It was a deep blue sapphire, cut into a strange shape, set into silver. It radiated a deep color in the warm sunshine, matching my pearl dress perfectly.

"Shall I ask my lord to approach?"

"Indeed. I should like to thank him for his gift."

I had entertained many diplomats and visitors from other countries arriving with costly gifts. Vague questions entered my head about this particular diplomat, but they left just as quickly. Another fanfare sounded, and this time a procession appeared. They looked like soldiers, men-at-arms, menservants and pages—the sort of people an aristocrat would have traveling with him.

The unknown personage was the last to appear. Like his entourage, he was attired in white. But his tunic came down to his ankles, the long sleeves adorned with fashionable jagged edges. He wore a stylish hat with a piece of material hanging down from it, protecting him from the dust of his journey. Altogether, he looked exotic and foreign, perhaps Italian. Perhaps from a place further to the east. I could not place him as he came closer. He exuded a scent of nutmeg and almonds, with a hint of exotic spices.

As I inhaled deeply, I remembered where I had encountered it before.

But now, the herald was announcing the aristocrat's name:

Philippe de Savoy, Count of Geneva.

He bowed and smiled as he held out his hand to take mine.

Then our eyes met.

Of course. His ruse was perfect, for no one would dare challenge a lord of such obvious means.

I swallowed.

The sounds in that bustling hall faded away as he straightened and we faced each other.

"Madam, I have a long journey to make, and I wondered if you would be good enough to give me some advice. I understand that stormy weather may blow in from Pontoise, and I wanted to know whether Rouen would provide a goodly place of shelter."

"No," I replied.

His eyebrows shot up. Silently he proffered his arm so that I had to leave the dais and walk into the hall with him.

His timing was perfect, for the servants were setting up the tables for the midday meal, and we stole some private moments together amidst the hubbub. He led me to an unoccupied window seat: "My sweet, are you sure?"

I was silent.

He took my hand. "My flower, I know how hard this is for you. But I have everything ready. My groom is outside waiting with an Arabian mare. I have spare clothes. You need only throw this cloak over your gown and we can leave."

I jerked away.

"I should have told you before," he murmured.

I clasped my shaking hands together.

"I have more people stationed outside Rouen waiting for us to arrive. You would be safe from your husband. There are many places where I could hide you."

"No," I interposed, looking down.

He waited, taking my hand in his.

After a long moment, I lifted my head. "I cannot go with you."

Abruptly, he let go of me. "Is it because I'm the son of a blacksmith?"

I put a hand on his sleeve. "You could not take me and three children."

"You promised to marry me."

"I cannot leave my children."

"We would have our own children."

I shook my head as I took his hand and kissed it. "If I had no children, I would go with you in a heartbeat."

A sound drowned out our conversation. A rumble of hooves. A fanfare sounded, and a shout went up. The men of the garrison, dicing and lounging in the shade of the trees outside, now scrambled to their feet, straightened their tunics, grabbed their weapons, and lined up in formation along the castle walls.

"They're back!" someone shouted. A roar answered.

His face turned as white as his tunic. "You will not come with me?"

"I cannot."

"You have my ring?" He dug into his tunic and produced another sapphire ring, quickly showing me how his ring fit around mine.

"If you change your mind, send your most trusty messenger to me with this ring. If it fits mine, I will know it comes from you."

"Where should I send the ring?"

"The Medici bank of Florence. They will get a message to me. There is a branch in every big city, including Paris and London."

He bowed low, took my hand, and kissed it. "Always at your service and ever devotedly yours." Then he abruptly pulled away, ran outside, vaulted onto his gelding, and rode off before I had time to breathe.

I ran to the window. In the distance I could make out Richard's pennant bearing his white lion.

Blaybourne rode straight for Richard; my heart slammed against my ribs. He drew his white horse level with Richard's black one, bowed low, and commenced a conversation. Moments later, Richard raised his gauntlet in salutation as the Count of Geneva and his entourage set off south, towards Paris.

I watched and watched until I could see him no more, my mind reeling.

But scarcely had I time to think. I sent orders to the cooks to prepare a more elaborate feast, and for the steward to bring up pipes of the best wine from the cellars. Everyone flooded back to the castle to greet the governor of Normandy and to hear news of the Pontoise campaign.

I slipped upstairs to the solar where Jenet bathed my tear-stained face with rosewater, re-did my hair, and rearranged my headdress. On impulse, I went to the *prie-dieu* in the corner of my chamber, closed my eyes, and knelt to pray.

Half an hour later, I made my way down to the great hall, into a noisy din of hundreds of guests drinking the health of the governor of Normandy. As I arrived, there was a sudden hush. The men rose and bowed.

My eyes met Richard's. He looked thinner than before, the hard exercise of the previous five weeks showing off a new muscular leanness. I'd never found him so attractive and was overcome with sorrow at what I'd done.

Richard came forward and, taking my hand, courteously led me to the seat beside him.

"Cis," he murmured, as he eyed my pearl-encrusted, blue-grey gown with its yards of billowing silk. "You look ravishing." He kissed me lightly on the cheek, and whispered into my ear, "I can hardly wait until tonight."

And then he turned and resumed his conversation with a gentleman sitting near him.

My hands shook as I sipped my wine.

At length, Richard turned towards me.

"Tell me about the campaign," I said. And so Richard spent the rest of the meal discussing tactics while I asked many questions.

A fanfare of trumpets sounded, heralding a toast. Richard rose, and I rose, forcing a smile onto my face. The whole hall shook as everyone lifted their cups and toasted the newly arrived Duke and his Duchess.

Afterwards, Richard and I, followed by the ladies and their husbands, the army, and the townspeople, rode down into the town of Rouen to celebrate a solemn Mass of thanksgiving in the cathedral. Then we went back to the castle, where the feasting and merrymaking went on for hours.

I collapsed into an exhausted sleep late that night. Afterwards, I was ill for a week. Every morning brought with it the painful knowledge that I would never see Blaybourne again, and that I'd hurt a good man who loved and trusted me.

I sat on a seat beside the bathing pool, near to where we'd had our tryst, unable to prevent the tears from trickling down my cheeks. I could see him, hear his voice, smell his scent.

Richard frowned and shot several glances at me as he paced up and down. "You have loyal friends here at Rouen. I have asked everyone what is wrong with you, and I get the same response: They avert their eyes, say you will get better in God's good time, and then change the subject."

I wiped away my tears with the tips of my fingers.

"As your husband, I have a right to know what is going on."

I studied my slippers. "I can't explain."

Richard gently tilted my face so that my eyes met his. His eyes gazed back, darkly. "What can't you explain?"

My head drooped as I drew a line in the dust with the toe of my slipper.

"You had an affair with another man."

My head jerked up. As my eyes met Richard's, he flushed.

"It's true! Christ on the Cross!"

He drew his sword, went to a nearby tree, and whacked it. I recoiled.

The spear-pointed diamond that hung from his gold collar jumped and glared at me in the harsh sunlight.

Richard turned round, his face taut, his mouth snarling. "How could you?"

I squeezed my folded arms against my chest.

He thrust his sword back into the scabbard, grabbed me, and jerked my head back. "Don't I mean anything to you? What about our marriage vows? What about our children?"

I stared back, trying not to see his pain, when suddenly he let go.

I clutched at the wooden bench to prevent myself from falling, then got to my feet.

"If you knew how many times I tried. How many times I walked away. How many times I tried to forget about him."

"So you blame him? By God Almighty and all his saints, if I ever catch him, I'll flay him alive."

"You won't."

"I won't what?"

"Catch him," I murmured, looking down.

I looked up to find Richard glaring at me. A vein in his forehead was throbbing. "And how do you know that?" he said in an icy tone I'd never heard before.

I folded my arms. "I don't even know his name."

"You don't know his name? How could you lie with someone you don't know? Are you so fickle, so shallow, that you pick up anyone who happens along?"

I lifted my chin. "If I 'd been free, if I'd not been married and had you and three children to think of—"

"You were thinking of running off with him." He folded his arms and gazed at me keenly.

I turned away.

He drew his sword, and walked up and down for several minutes, whacking trees, hedges, anything that he came into contact with. Leaves, twigs and branches strewed the path. Then he sheathed his sword. "I would banish you now. I would lock you up. But I need your family."

I shivered. I had never heard such cold calculation from Richard before.

"You are a Neville," he spat. "There are political considerations. Salisbury is a loyal supporter. I am constantly in the position of struggling to make my voice heard on the king's council. I would be nowhere were it not for your brother's support. A scandal would make me the laughing stock of the whole court."

The color drained from my face.

"You didn't think of that, did you?" he snapped, thrusting his face into mine so that I felt the drops of his spittle as he bit each word off.

I stepped backwards.

"If your family were not so valuable to my political career, I would punish you as you deserve."

Blaybourne's voice filled my ears: *Would he lock you up?*

"Are you with child?"

I lowered my head.

"You spend days, nay, weeks in that misbegotten knave's arms. And you expect me to accept his bastard!" He looked around. "It happened here, didn't it?" His eye caught the door in the yew hedge through which the private garden with the turf seat could be seen. He reached out and held my arm in a vice-like grip. "It was on that turf seat wasn't it? It was in this garden where you spent your time."

"One night," I murmured.

He twisted me around. "Look at me, damn you. What did you say?"

"It was only one night."

"Ha! So you wish it had been more."

He grabbed me around the waist with one hand, while with the other hand he gripped my chin so that I was forced to look at him. We gazed at each other in dead silence for several minutes.

"Damn you, Cis," he said between his teeth, letting go of me so suddenly, I crumpled into a heap.

"I am cursed!" he shouted over and over again.

I crossed myself. Was Lisette's curse coming true? I wiped the dust from my clothes and hair and rose. "I am here, Richard. I have not gone."

"Aye, but you lie to me. What is his name?"

An image of Blaybourne filled my mind. I couldn't give him away. I resented Richard for assuming he had a right to know my private thoughts and feelings. Was I to have no space to call my own in this marriage? Blaybourne would be my space.

"I think you know, but for some reason, you won't tell me. Come, my love, out with it."

"No."

"No, you don't know? Or, no, you're not telling?"

I stared at the ground.

Richard sprang forward and lifted me up in his arms, holding me in a vise. "You know I could lock you up. I could forbid you to see the children. I could starve you to death."

I shook, then looked him full in the face. "But you cannot make me talk."

He slapped me hard across the cheek. He grabbed me by the arm as I crumpled to my knees, holding my throbbing face.

"Woman. You will speak. I asked you a question. What is the knave's name?"

"I will never tell you."

"You love him as much as that? You would risk all?"

"Yes." I moved to the other side of the seat. "I have never loved anyone before. When you met me after all those years, you were experienced, but I was not. I married you because I had to. I had no notion of what love was like, until now. Here I am. You can do with me as you please. My heart is broken. I don't much care what happens to me now."

Richard moved swiftly to prevent me escaping and imprisoned me against a tree by putting his arms on either side of me. I closed my eyes, but could not get away from him. I could smell the leathery scent of his sweat, and hear his heavy breathing.

"Are you with child?"

I was silent.

He tore himself away. "I cannot believe you would do this!" He slumped onto the bench and put his face in his hands.

I stared at him, still backed up against the tree. I did not dare move.

Chapter 6
September 1441 to April 1442

When Richard found out that I was indeed carrying another's child, he was not best pleased. He did not shout or carry on, but compressed his lips into a thin line. Thereafter, although scrupulously courteous, he was cold.

It didn't help when the quarterly bills came due at Michaelmas, for they were unusually high. During Richard's absence, I'd been unable to resist all the lovely luxuries the merchants of Rouen kept bringing to the castle. Richard did not bother with a confrontation. Instead, he sent a note saying that he'd hired a Master Elbeuf to be comptroller of the household, and if I needed money, I was to consult him. This was a clever way for Richard to keep watch on me, for if he knew exactly how I spent my allowance, he'd know how I was spending my time. I couldn't argue with his logic.

Things continued in this uneasy state through October; then little Henry sickened as the first frosts appeared. He died on All Hallows Eve, aged eight months. Truth to tell, I'd never paid much attention to the child, being so occupied with getting the entire household to Rouen shortly after his birth, and then being caught up in my affair of the heart. Now he was dead, and Richard lost his heir.

As I sat there with my hand on Henry's cold cheek, there was a stir, a glint from the diamond, and Richard arrived. He cleared the room with a look and went up to me.

"Well?" he demanded coldly.

"I do not know what happened."

"You don't know. Why not?"

"He was never strong."

"No, he was not. And whose fault was that?"

He came over and gripped my chin with his fingers, so that I was forced to look into his eyes, hard and steely.

"I'm sorry," I whispered.

"You should be. You have been extremely careless, madam, in the care of my son. Riding off to Lincoln in your condition, when you were six months gone with him."

"I had to go to Mama's funeral."

"You should have waited until he was born to pay your respects to your lady mother. If you had done as I'd asked and stayed at Fotheringhay, he would have been stronger. And now we would not be dealing with the death of my heir."

Henry was buried in the Abbey of Saint-Ouen.

After that, I did not see Richard for several weeks. As winter intensified its grip, I spent my days sitting in front of the often-smoking fire, cuddling Joan on my lap. One day Joan could not stop coughing. I thought she had a bad cold, but she started wheezing and making gurgling noises. I doused the fire, but it made no difference. I tried to force syrup down her convulsing throat, but most of it spilled onto her clothes. After a long struggle, she turned blue and expired. She was three and a half.

I clutched Joan to my breast while tears rolled down my cheeks. When the priest came, they forced me to drink a draught of poppy juice because I would not hand her over for the last rites.

When I came to, I ran to the window. Someone—it was Richard—was quick enough to grab me. I twisted my head to look at him.

"Let me die."

"What of your immortal soul? That sin would land you in the fires of damnation."

Everything went black.

When I came to, I was lying in bed and someone was holding my hand. As I gradually surfaced, something glinted through my closed eyelids. Richard sat on a stool by my bed.

His face looked grey, new lines carving the flesh around his eyes and mouth.

"You've come back."

I raised myself up and looked around. "Why am I not dead? I should be."

Richard turned his head; the room filled with the sounds of people leaving. He sat on the bed and took me in his arms. "I thought we'd lost you," he murmured, holding me close.

I felt the diamond hard against my bosom. I gently pulled back and looked at him. "But why do you want me? I've wronged you."

"Cis!" he exclaimed, putting his hands on my shoulders and giving me a shake. He stopped abruptly as my eyes filled with tears. There was silence for many moments. "Don't you see how much I love you? I want you, not someone else." He kissed me gently on the lips.

"But I hurt you."

"You've been punished enough." And rising, he dashed a hand across his eyes, turned on his heel, and left.

I didn't see him again for many weeks. We buried Joan in the chapel of Saint Romain, in the castle, so that I could visit her every day.

I made a slow recovery. By some miracle, I didn't lose my child. Every day, I went with Margaret to visit Joan to pray for her soul. Every evening, I went to confession and confessed my sins to Père André, the castle chaplain. It took much time, but in the end I told him the whole story.

Père André was a wise man and a good priest. He did not fob me off with a few *Aves* here, a few *Paternosters* there. He systematically went over my sins, discussing them at great length. Then he recommended books that I should read, starting with *The Confessions of Saint Augustine*. But the most important thing he taught me was how to pray. I spent many hours on my knees praying during the winter and spring of 1442. That was how I gradually recovered my sanity.

"My lady, do you want to see your son?" Annette de Caux's voice disturbed my reverie. Annette had stayed on after Henry's death, suckling her own child and acting as a governess for little Nan. Now I engaged her as wet nurse for the new baby.

"Not until I've seen my lord husband."

And there he was, standing in the doorway. I'd scarcely seen him since the day he'd pulled me back from the gates of hell.

Annette, Jenet, and the other women hurriedly bobbed their curtsies and left while Richard came over and stood by the side of the bed.

"A son," he said, "You gave him a son."

I was silent.

"Are you going to send word to him?"

"Do you want me to?"

Richard sighed and sat down on the bed. "At least you chose a nobleman. The master sergeant of the garrison told me that one of the archers was a nobleman of the House of Savoy. He disappeared the day I arrived."

I fixed my eyes on Richard's face. Did he know anything else? Did he know he'd spoken with my lover? How would he feel if he knew Blaybourne was a peasant?

"I'll leave with the baby if you wish."

Richard stared.

"Or, I could stay with you," I murmured hastily, trying to soften his stony look.

"Of course you're staying with me!" he shouted, seizing me by the shoulders. "I would never let you go. You know that."

"Perhaps you would like another wife."

"Do you want to leave me?"

I looked at my long-suffering husband as though I were seeing him for the first time. He wasn't tall, but he wasn't fat either. He wasn't exceeding graceful, but he wasn't uncouth. The recent lines around his eyes and mouth made his face more interesting, less bland. His eyes were his best feature, a clear blue-grey that reflected his every mood.

I hung my head. How stupid I'd been. Kind husbands who stood by you in a crisis were a rarity. And what of Nan? She needed me. It was my duty to hold my family together. I lifted my eyes and put my hand into his.

Richard wrapped his fingers around mine and held on tightly.

I lowered my lashes. Blaybourne seemed so dim and far away. Would I have been welcome if I'd gone to him? Who was he anyway? I wasn't sure if I believed him to be a powerful nobleman, a scholar, or a humble archer. I opened my eyes. "I would rather stay."

Richard drew me close. "The greatest wish I have is for my wife to love me. Could you?" His eyes bored into mine, going darker as they gazed at me.

I touched his cheek lightly with my finger, all hesitations gone. "Yes," I breathed, and he kissed me with more abandon than he ever had before.

"I could never let you go," he murmured over and over.

I leaned my head against his chest and frowned. "But what of the baby?" I asked hesitantly.

Richard stiffened. "Where is it?" he demanded, pulling away and rising.

"I don't know."

"You don't know?" Richard's eyebrows drew together.

"I didn't want to see him until I'd talked with you first."

"I see." Richard went to the door and signaled to Annette to bring the child.

"Would you like to hold him, my lady?" asked Annette.

I looked at Richard. Richard went over to look at the child. "He's big and perfectly formed. He seems robust and healthy. He'd be a good fighter." He fingered his beard. "You know what this means, of course."

I shook my head.

"If I say nothing, he becomes my heir."
I clasped my hands. "Is that what you want?"

About the Author

Cynthia Sally Haggard was born and raised in Surrey, England. About thirty years ago she came to the United States and has lived there ever since in the Mid-Atlantic region. She has had four careers, violinist, cognitive scientist, medical writer and novelist. Yes, she is related to H. Rider Haggard, the author of SHE and KING SOLOMONS'S MINES. (He was a younger brother of her great-grandfather.) She got into novel writing by accident, when an instructor announced one day that each member of his class had to produce five pages of their next novel. She took a deep breath and began. She hasn't stopped since.

Connect with me online at my blog: http://spunstories.com/

Author's Note

Thwarted Queen is set in the hundred years that led up to the Reformation in England. During Cecylee's lifetime from 1415 to 1495, the church in England was ruled by the Pope in Rome, as it had been for nearly one thousand years. The Wars of the Roses were therefore not about religion, for everyone worshipped in the same way.

Thwarted Queen naturally divides into four books. *Book One: The Bride Price* is about Cecylee's girlhood. *Book Two: One Seed Sown* is about her love-affair with Blaybourne. *Book Three: The Gilded Cage* is about Richard of York's political career from 1445 to his death in 1460, and covers the opening of the Wars of the Roses. *Book Four: Two Murders Reaped* is about Cecylee's actions in old age, and how she may have had a hand in the murder of the two little princes in the Tower. I used different points of view to convey mood and setting. *The Bride Price* is written in first-person present to capture the freshness of a young girl's voice. *One Seed Sown* is written in first-person past to make Cecylee seem older and more mature. *The Gilded Cage* had to be written in third-person to capture all of the different voices and the complexity of Richard's political life. *Two Murders Reaped* is written in first person past, to capture the voice of the old woman that Cecylee became.

     In thinking about Cecylee and what kind of person she must have been to have lead the kind of life you have just read about, I decided I needed a heroine. I needed someone that Cecylee could emulate both as an impressionable young girl and as an older woman. I chose Queen Alainor of Aquitaine, known as Eleanor of Aquitaine to modern readers. She was a real person who lived between 1120 and 1204. Like Cecylee, she lived to a great age and was the mother of two Kings of England; Richard I *Coeur de Lion* (*the Lionheart*), who reigned from 1189 to 1199, and King John, who reigned from 1199 to 1216. She repeatedly broke the rules of what was considered seemly behavior for ladies. Her first act of independence came when she divorced her first husband – Louis VII of France – and married Henry Plantagenet, who became Henry II of England. Later on, after she inspired her sons to rebel against her husband, he locked her up for sixteen years. However, she outlived him, and was let out of prison by her son Richard I. She ruled England for King Richard during his many absences, and won a reputation for fair dealing and wise judgement at the many assizes she held throughout the country. I saw in her the perfect role model for the young and subversive Cecylee.

     Why didn't I choose Joan of Arc to be Cecylee's heroine? Because she didn't make her appearance until 1429, and the story of Cecylee's girlhood in *Thwarted Queen* covers the years 1424-1425.

     The most controversial part of Cecylee's early life is her betrothal in October 1424. Most historians think she married Richard at that point, and the young couple went to live at the court of King Henry VI. Though this is certainly possible, I made the ceremony a betrothal because I found it hard to believe that Cecylee didn't produce any children for fourteen years. Cecylee was fecund, her children were born in 1438, 1439, 1441, 1442, 1443, 1444, 1446, 1447, 1448,

1449, 1450, 1452 and 1455. Although she was only nine years old in 1424, she could have started producing children by 1430, when she was fourteen turning fifteen. I reasoned that she was not living with Richard until 1437 at the earliest, and that the reason she wasn't living with Richard was because she wasn't married to him.

In thinking about who might have stopped the marriage, I noticed that her father died in 1425 when she was ten years old, and that Richard's wardship passed into her mother's hands. The person most likely to have prevented this marriage was Cecylee's mother Countess Joan. The reason for doing so probably stemmed from the fact that Cecylee was the youngest daughter and all of Countess Joan's other daughters had already been married off and left the family. It is also possible that Countess Joan did not like Richard. I used a fictional episode toward the end of *Book One: The Bride Price* to motivate her dislike.

It seems that Countess Joan was interested in literature. She may have leant two books to King Henry V (her half-grand-nephew) when he went to fight the French at the Battle of Agincourt. And Hoccleve may have dedicated one of his books to her. It is true that Geoffrey Chaucer was Countess Joan's uncle-by-marriage and so she probably owned some of the original manuscripts, which have since disappeared. I do not know if Countess Joan held a reading circle, but it would have been typical of the time period for her to do so. I understand that Abbesses would ride from one great house to another with provocative manuscripts tucked away in their saddle-bags, using the reading circles as a forum for subversive activity, rather like the women writers of Afghanistan who carried on under the guise of sewing circles, as described in *The Sewing Circles of Herat*. (Anyone who has read the *Wife of Bath's Tale* knows how subversive it is.) Apart from the *Wife of Bath*, I have also included some lines from Chaucer's *Parliament of Fowls* and the opening of *The Owl and the Nightingale* – which was written anonymously in around 1272 – to give a flavor of the times and some idea of the kind of literature they were reading. Of course I could not quote Shakespeare, as he was not born until 1564.

The songs were also chosen to be representative of the period. Blaybourne's chanson *Plus Bele que Flor* (More Lovely Than A Flower), and Cecylee's songs *I Cannot Help It If I Rarely Sing* and *This Lovely Star Of The Sea* come from the Montpellier Codex of the 13th century. It is quite possible that people continued to sing these songs well into the 15th century, making changes as they went along.

You may wonder why I chose to believe the tale of Cecylee's affair with an archer on the Rouen garrison. After all, Anne Easter Smith, who has written her own novel about Cecylee, dismisses it out of hand. I believed it both because it had a ring of truth to it, and because it explains so many things. It explains, for example, why Cecylee helped to nullify Edward IV's will shortly after his death, and why Richard III repeatedly sought his mother's counsel and seemed to have had a much closer relationship with her than Edward IV ever did. It also explains Richard of York's actions, why he had a sumptuous christening ceremony for his second surviving son Rutland, but not for Edward. And why he chose to exile himself to Ireland with Rutland, but not Edward. During that moment of crisis in 1459 when everything seemed lost, it is interesting that Edward sat it out in Calais with his mother's relatives, rather than being by Richard of York's side.

Of course, Cecylee's lover Blaybourne presented his own set of problems. Scarcely anything is known about him, except that he was an archer on the Rouen garrison during the summer of 1441 when Cecylee's husband Richard was away campaigning against the French in Pontoise. I was forced to make up everything about his life and circumstances and I tried to draw a character who was plausible for the fifteenth century, making him someone who would have gotten his opportunities in life from his education in a monastery.

To give a cultural read on the risks that Cecylee was taking, I included two stories about jealous husbands and the ways in which they punished their wives. Black Fulk, more commonly known in Anjou as *Foulques Nerra*, was Count of Anjou from 987, when he was around fifteen years old, until his death in 1040. He had a violent temperament, so the story that he burned his first wife Helizabeth in the market square at Angers after discovering her in bed with a lover, may well be true.

When twenty-one-year-old Parisina (or Laura) Malatesta was discovered in bed with her twenty-year-old stepson Ugo d'Este, her husband (and his father) Niccolo III d'Este ordered their executions. They were beheaded on May 21, 1425, when Cecylee had just turned ten.

Beginning with *Book Three: The Gilded Cage*, the novel becomes much more factually-based as Cecylee emerges from the shadows. I followed the opinions of historians Alison Weir and Michael K. Jones in trying to reconstruct this period, especially Alison Weir's *The Wars of the Roses* and *The Princes in the Tower*, and Michael K. Jones' *Bosworth 1485: The Psychology of Battle*.

It is true that Cecylee's six-year-old daughter was married off in 1446. I do not know if this was Richard's way of punishing his wife for taking a lover, but Nan was forced to marry someone who was notorious for his cruelty. If you are one of those readers wondering why a six-year-old bride would be more useful than an older girl - given that she would not be able to bear children for several years - you have to remember that these girls were used as pawns in huge land transfers. The reason for marrying a young child now rather than later was because the family she was marrying into was impatient to acquire the wealth of the land that she brought as a dowry.

Obviously, there must have been a huge problem of child abuse, for these young girls were taken from their families, and sent off to live with their in-laws at the time of marriage. Legally, the husband became the child-bride's liege lord, which meant that he had total control over her. The child-bride was thrust upon the mercy of her husband and in-laws, in a situation that is not unlike the one that occurs in India today. This practice was not uncommon six hundred years ago. In *Thwarted Queen* there are at least two other examples; Cecylee's sister Alainor, who was forced into a marriage when she was five years old. When her 18-year-old bridegroom died, she was married to the Earl of Northumberland's heir when she was seven. The other example is Richard's sister Isabel who was married when she was about four years old to Sir Thomas Grey. That marriage was annulled for reasons that are not clear; but it is possible that Isabel was badly treated. By contrast, if the young girl was betrothed, she continued to be under the jurisdiction of her parents and lived with her family of origin until the marriage took place.

It is not known what happened to the little princes in the Tower (the sons and heirs of Edward IV). In trying to reconstruct what happened I have followed the ideas of Alison Weir in her *The Princes in the Tower*. However, not all historians agree that Richard III murdered his nephews, so I have given an alternative explanation at the end of the novel, in which I suggest that the younger brother, Richard, Duke of York, was smuggled out of the country and lived in Burgundy. If you are wondering why everyone is so certain that the elder brother, Edward V died in the Tower, it is because there are records showing that the poor young man was suffering from a severe ear infection in the summer of 1483. Without modern medicine, it is almost certain that his condition would have killed him within the year.

A couple of incidents in *Thwarted Queen* are based on the testimony of people alive at the time. Cecylee's tirade against Edward IV – in which she publicly announces he is illegitimate – is based on what Dominic Mancini, an Italian diplomat of the time, wrote. I have followed the historian Michael K. Jones' opinion that Cecylee was exiled to Berkhamsted Castle in March of 1469, and thus Cecylee's explosion occurred shortly beforehand. Echoes of this can be seen in Shakespeare's *Richard III*, except that in the play Cecylee's tirade is directed against Richard III. Shakespeare's play can be treated as propaganda on behalf of the Tudors. He did everything he could to blacken the character of

Richard III, and so one can almost treat the play as a mirror-image of what actually occurred.

The other incident is Edward's marriage to Lady Eleanor Butler. This is based upon the testimony of Robert Stillington, Bishop of Bath and Wells. It is not known when the marriage actually took place, but I have set it in April 1462, because it gave a plausible time-frame for Lady Eleanor to have had a child before Edward met Elisabeth Woodville, whom he married two years later in May 1464. As in the novel, these facts did not come to light until after Edward's death. People at the time had difficulty believing this story because it was so obviously in Richard of Gloucester's interests to claim that Edward's marriage to Elisabeth Woodville was bigamous. However, the story had the ring of plausibility for me, because Edward was a notorious womanizer who may have been attracted to older widows. (Both Elisabeth Woodville and Eleanor Talbot were Lancastrian widows. Elisabeth Woodville was five years older than Edward, and Eleanor Butler would have been about seven years older.)

As far as I know, there is no evidence that Cecylee ever referred to her daughter-in-law as *The Serpent*, though it is true that she was dismayed by Edward's marriage and the two ladies seemed not to have liked each other. I picked that particular nickname because I felt it conveyed volumes about how Cecylee felt about Edward's Queen. Elisabeth's name for Cecylee, *good mother*, is meant to sound disrespectful. It is meant to sound like *Goodwife*, which although it was a polite form of address for women, only applied to those of the lowest social classes. By calling Cecylee *good mother*, rather than *Madam*, Elisabeth conveyed her animosity towards her mother-in-law. The encounters between Cecylee and Queen Elisabeth are fictional, but are based on fact, such as the Queen's rapacious relatives wiping the aristocratic marriage market clean and Cecylee's resulting problems in trying to find suitable marriage partners for her children. Cecylee did style herself *Queen By Right* and she did move into the Queen's apartments, forcing her son Edward to build a separate wing for his new wife. The speech in which she tells Edward off about his marriage is based upon Sir Thomas More's account as reported by Michael K. Jones.

Writing about the past forces historical novelists to confront the fraught issue of dates of birth. It is often difficult to pin an age on a person, especially minor female characters, because dates of birth were not systematically recorded. The reader should therefore take the ages of most of the characters as approximations.

Documents from the time provided a fascinating glimpse of Cecylee's life in her later years. *Orders and Rules of the Princess Cecill* and *The Rules of the House* show a strong-minded yet kind woman running a tight ship at Berkhamsted Castle. I hope you enjoyed the quotations from these sources. In her will of 1495, Cecylee makes reference to two nearby convents:

> *"Also I geve to the house of Assherugge a chesibule and 2 tunicles of crymsyn damaske embrawdered with thre albes. Also I geve to the house of Saint Margaretes twoo auter clothes with a crucifix and a vestiment of grene vellet..."*

I haven't been able to trace a convent of Saint Margaret, but there was a convent at Ashridge, about four miles from Berkhamsted castle, and so I chose to place Cecylee's friends from her later years there. (In the fifteenth century, most people didn't think twice about walking four miles).

Such documents also give us clues to how things were pronounced. In Cecylee's will of 1495, for example, she refers to Fotheringhay as "Fodringhey", so I used that pronunciation in the scene where Richard talks about his favorite residence to Queen Marguerite d'Anjou.

Lastly, readers may wonder how I came to choose the name *Cecylee*. Not wanting to get caught up in the Cecily/Cicely controversy, I thought it would be interesting to see how Cecylee herself spelt her name. Her will is in the public domain, and it seems that she signed it *Cecylee*. However, her handwriting is extremely difficult to read – it looks like the signature of someone who does not write much – so it is possible that she actually spelled her name *Cecylle*. In the fifteenth century spelling varied widely and great ladies like Cecylee usually dictated their letters and papers to scribes who came from different regions of the country and spelled things differently. According to the Richard III society, Cecylee in her lifetime was addressed as *Cecill, Cecille, Cecyll* but the most usual form of the name was *Cecylee*. And so I went with that version of the name, knowing that it would be easy for English-speaking readers to figure out how to pronounce it. (It is pronounced in the exact same way as the more modern spelling of the name, *Cecily*.) If I had been writing for French readers, I probably would have called her *Cecylle*, because that is closer to the French version of the name *Cécile*.

It was an honor as well as great fun to have Cecylee materialize from the fifteenth century and talk to me about her life. I hope you enjoyed reading this novel as much as I enjoyed writing it.

Cynthia Sally Haggard
Washington D. C., 2011.

Below is a selection of sources I used in researching *Thwarted Queen*, followed by a list of characters in the novel.

Books

Amt, Emilie (1992). *Women's Lives in Medieval Europe: A Sourcebook.*

Ankarloo, Bengt and Stuart Clark (2002). *Witchcraft and Magic in Europe. Volume 3: The Middle Ages.*

Anonymous 4. *Love's Illusion: Music from the Montpellier Codex, 13th century.*

Baldwin, David (2004). *Elizabeth Woodville: Mother of the Princes in the Tower.*

Cartidge, Neil (2001). *The Owl and the Nightingale: Text and Translation.* University of Exeter Press.

Chaucer, Geoffrey (1382/2004). *The Parliament of Birds.* Hesperus Press.

Chantilly, Musée Condé, Jean Longnon, Raymond Cazelles (1489/1989). *The Très Riches Heures of Jean, Duc de Berry.*

Cobb, John Wolstenholme (1883/2008). History & Antiquities of Berkhamsted.

Gies, Frances (1991). *Life in a Medieval Village*

Gies, Frances (1998). *A Medieval Family: The Pastons of Fifteenth-Century England.*

Hardy, Robert (1992). *Longbow: A Social and Military History.*

Houston, Mary G. (1996). *Medieval Costume in England and France: The 13th, 14th and 15th centuries.*

Jones, Michael K. (2003). *Bosworth 1485: The Psychology of a Battle* (Revealing History Series).

Landsberg, Sylvia (2003). *The Medieval Garden.*

Parlett, David (1991). *A History of Card Games.*

Ross, Charles (1998). *Edward IV* (The English Monarchs Series).

Smith, A. H. (1978). *Three Northumbrian Poems.* (Exeter Medieval Texts and Studies).
    Exeter University Press.

Weir, Alison (1995). *The Princes in the Tower.*

Weir, Alison (1996). *The Wars of the Roses.*

Weir, Alison (2009). *Mistress of the Monarchy: The Life of Katherine Swynford, Duchess of Lancaster.*

Whiteman, Robin and Rob Talbot Brother (1996). *Brother Cadfael's Herb Garden: An Illustrated Companion to Medieval Plants and Their Uses.*

Characters

(in order of appearance)

LADY CECYLEE NEVILLE, DUCHESS OF YORK "CIS" (born 1415).

JOAN DE BEAUFORT, COUNTESS OF WESTMORLAND (born circa 1379, died 1440). Cecylee's mother, and daughter of John of Gaunt and his third wife Catrine de Roet. Married (a) Robert Ferrers, 5th Baron Boteler of Wem (died circa 1395), and (b) Ralph de Neville, 1st Earl of Westmorland.

JOHN PLANTAGENET, DUKE OF BEDFORD (1389-1435) younger brother to Henry V of England, uncle to Henry VI. Negotiated marriage between Richard, Duke of York and Cecylee Neville. Married (a) Anne of Burgundy (died 1432), and (b) Jacquetta de St Pol.

RALPH DE NEVILLE, 1st EARL OF WESTMORLAND (born circa 1363, died 1425). Cecylee's father. Married (a) Margaret de Stafford (died circa 1395), and (b) Joan de Beaufort. His marriage with Countess Joan took place in November 1396.

HUMPHREY PLANTAGENET, DUKE OF GLOUCESTER (1390-1447), younger brother of John, Duke of Bedford. Married (a) Jacqueline of Hainault (marriage annulled in 1428), and (b) Eleanor Cobham.

HENRY VI, KING OF ENGLAND (born 1422). Only son and heir of Henry V, the victor of Agincourt in 1415.

RICHARD PLANTAGENET, "DICKON" (born 1411), 3RD DUKE OF YORK from 1415, EARL OF MARCH from 1425, EARL OF CAMBRIDGE and EARL OF ULSTER from 1432. Cecylee's intended, they were betrothed on October 18, 1424 and married circa 1437.

GEOFFREY CHAUCER (born circa 1340, died between 1400 and 1402). Married Philippa de Roet, sister to Catrine de Roet, Cecylee's grandmother. The greatest poet of his day, he is most famous for THE CANTERBURY TALES. In his day, he was also famous for THE

PARLIAMENT OF THE FOWLS, and THE BOOK
OF THE DUCHESS, written circa 1469 to
commemorate the death of his patron's wife, Blanche of
Lancaster, from the plague.

LADY MARY DE FERRERS (born 1394). Cecylee's half-
sister, younger daughter of Joan de Beaufort and Robert
Ferrers, married to her stepbrother Sir Ralph Neville The
Older , a younger son of Ralph Neville, 1st Earl of
Westmorland and Margaret Stafford.

LADY ANNE NEVILLE (born circa 1411). Cecylee's sister,
married to Humphrey, 6th Earl of Stafford, later Duke of
Buckingham.

LADY CATRINE DE NEVILLE "CATH" (born circa
1397). Cecylee's sister, married four times to (a) John de
Mowbray, 2nd Duke of Norfolk, (b) Sir Thomas
Strangeways, (c) John, Viscount Beaumont, and (d) Sir
John Woodville.

ELEANOR "ALAINOR", DUCHESS OF AQUITAINE
(1120-1204) mother of King Richard I *The Lionheart* and
King John. Cecylee's heroine, she divorced her first
husband to marry her second.

CATRINE DE ROET (1350-1404), also known as Lady
Katherine Swynford. Cecylee's grandmother, and
Countess Joan's mother. She married (a) Sir Hugh
Swynford, and (b) John of Gaunt.

LOUIS VII, King of France (1120-1180), the first husband
of Alainor or Eleanor of Aquitaine.

HENRY OF ANJOU (1133-1189), HENRY II OF
ENGLAND from 1154, the second husband of Eleanor
of Aquitaine.

HUMPHREY STAFFORD 6th EARL STAFFORD
(1402-1460), married to Cecylee's sister Anne.

LADY ELIZABETH DE FERRERS "BESS", (born 1393).
Cecylee's half-sister, elder daughter of Joan de Beaufort
and Robert Ferrers, married to John de Greystoke, 4th
Baron Greystoke.

LADY JEHANE DE NEVILLE (born circa 1398), a nun at
Barking Abbey in Essex.

LADY ALAINOR DE NEVILLE (born circa 1407), married to Henry Percy, 2nd Earl of Northumberland at the age of seven.

RICHARD NEVILLE, BARON MONTACUTE "SALISBURY" (1400-1460) 5th EARL OF SALISBURY from 1428 . Eldest son of Joan de Beaufort and Ralph Neville, 1st Earl of Westmorland. Baron Montacute and Earl of Salisbury in right of his wife, Alice de Montacute, the wealthy heiress to the Salisbury title and lands.

ALICE DE MONTACUTE, COUNTESS OF SALISBURY (born circa 1408), wife to Cecylee's eldest brother Richard Neville, Earl of Salisbury

LADY CECILY NEVILLE (born circa 1424), Cecylee's namesake niece, daughter of her eldest brother SALISBURY.

EDWARD NEVILLE, LORD BERGAVENNY (born circa 1417). Youngest child of Joan de Beaufort and Ralph Neville, 1st Earl of Westmorland. Lord Bergavenny in right of his wife, Elizabeth de Beauchamp.

LADY ELIZABETH DE BEAUCHAMP "LISBET" (born circa 1415), daughter of Isabel le Despencer, Countess of Worcester and Warwick and Richard de Beauchamp, 1st Earl of Worcester. The wealthy Worcester heiress was called "Lady of Bergavenny".

HUMPHREY STAFFORD (born circa 1424), Cecylee's nephew, son of her sister Anne.

LADY ISABEL PLANTAGENET (1409-1484), Richard of York's sister, married to Sir Thomas Grey at the age of four. The marriage was annulled, and she married Henry, Baron Bourchier in 1426.

ISABEL LE DESPENCER, COUNTESS OF WORCESTER AND WARWICK (1400-1439), married (a) Richard de Beauchamp, 1st Earl of Worcester and (b) Richard de Beauchamp 13th Earl of Warwick, and cousin to her first husband. She was Lady Lisbet's mother.

HENRY, CARDINAL BEAUFORT (born circa 1381, died 1447), brother to Countess Joan, younger son of John of Gaunt and Catrine de Roet.

LADY ANNE DE MORTIMER (1390-1411), eldest child of Roger Mortimer, granddaughter of Philippa, Countess of Ulster, great-granddaughter of Lionel of Antwerp, the second son of King Edward III of England. The only child of Roger Mortimer to have heirs, she bequeathed the wealthy Mortimer inheritance to her son Richard, Duke of York, Cecylee's husband. She was also mother to Richard's elder sister Isabel Plantagenet.

SIR RALPH NEVILLE THE OLDER (died 1458), younger son of Ralph Neville, 1st Earl of Westmorland and Margaret Stafford.

SIR JOHN NEVILLE (died 1423), eldest son of Ralph Neville, 1st Earl of Westmorland and Margaret Stafford.

SIR RALPH NEVILLE THE YOUNGER, 2nd EARL OF WESTMORLAND (born circa 1406, died circa 1484), son of Sir John Neville, and grandson of Ralph Neville, 1st Earl of Westmorland.

JOHN PLANTAGENET DUKE OF LANCASTER, "JOHN OF GAUNT" (1340-1399). The third son of King Edward III, he married (a) Blanche of Lancaster, (b) Constance of Castile (c) Catrine de Roet (Lady Katherine Swynford). By his first wife Blanche, he was the father of King Henry IV of England. By his second wife Constance, he was father to Queen Catherine of Castile. By his third wife Catrine, he was father to Joan de Beaufort and her three brothers. He was therefore Cecylee's grandfather.

EDWARD III, KING OF ENGLAND (1312-1377), reigned England from 1327 to 1377. Known for his consultative kingship, in which he kept his magnates happy by asking their advice on affairs of state, and by marrying his sons into the English aristocracy, he reigned peacefully for 50 years. Cecylee's great-grandfather.

LADY ELIZABETH PERCY (died 1437), daughter of Sir Henry Percy "Harry Hotspur", she was sister to Henry Percy 2nd Earl of Northumberland, the husband of Cecylee's sister Alainor.

SIR THOMAS GREY (dates unknown), was the namesake son of Sir Thomas Grey and Alice Neville, daughter to Ralph Neville, 1st Earl of Westmorland and Margaret Stafford. He was married to Isabel Plantagenet, sister of Richard, Duke of York in 1413, when she was four years old.

ABBESS MARGARET DE SWYNFORD (born circa 1363), daughter of Catrine de Roet and Sir Hugh Swynford. She was half-sister to Joan de Beaufort and Abbess of Barking Abbey.

ELIZABETH CHAUCER, (born circa 1363), daughter of Geoffrey Chaucer and Philippa de Roet, younger sister to Catrine de Roet. She was a nun at Barking Abbey.

ANICIUS MANLIUS SEVERINUS BOETHIUS "BOETHIUS" (circa 480-525 CE), a philosopher of the early 6th century.

CHRISTINE DE PIZAN (circa 1363-1430), famous for being Europe's first professional woman writer, she turned to writing on the death of her husband when she was 24 years old and had to support a household that consisted of her mother, her niece and her two children.

LADY JOAN PLANTAGENET (born circa 1438, died as a child), eldest child of Cecylee and Richard.

LADY ANNE PLANTAGENET, "NAN" (born 1439), second child of Cecylee and Richard.

LORD HENRY PLANTAGENET (born 1441, died as a child), third child of Cecylee and Richard.

HENRY BOURCHIER, 2ND COUNT OF EU, 5TH BARON BOURCHIER (1406-1483) 1ST VISCOUNT BOURCHIER from 1446, 1ST EARL OF ESSEX from 1461. Married from 1426 to Richard's sister Isabel.

LADY ELIZABETH HOWARD, COUNTESS OF OXFORD "BESS" (born circa 1411, died 1475), she was the daughter of Sir John Howard, 7th Lord Plaitz. She married John de Vere, 12th Earl of Oxford.

JOHN DE VERE, 12TH EARL OF OXFORD (1408-1462). One of Richard's generals, he fought the French during the Pontoise Campaign of 1441.

LADY MARGARET BEAUCHAMP, COUNTESS OF SHREWSBURY (1404-1468), eldest daughter of Richard de

Beauchamp, 13th Earl of Warwick and his first wife Elizabeth de Berkeley, she was married to John Talbot, 1st Earl of Shrewsbury.

JOHN TALBOT, 10TH BARON STRANGE OF BLACKMERE, 1ST EARL OF WATERFORD (1390-1453), 1ST EARL OF SHREWSBURY from 1442. He held Pontoise for the English while the French besieged it during the summer of 1441.

LADY ELIZABETH BEAUCHAMP "LISETTE" (born circa 1421, died 1480), youngest daughter of Richard de Beauchamp, 13th Earl of Warwick and his first wife Elizabeth de Berkeley, she was married to Cecylee's brother George, Lord Latimer.

GEORGE NEVILLE, 1ST BARON LATIMER (born circa 1414, died 1469), one of Cecylee's brothers. He succeeded to the title on the death of his half-uncle John Neville in 1430.

WILLIAM NEVILLE, LORD FAUCONBERG (born circa 1409, died 1463), 1ST EARL OF KENT from 1461, was one of Cecylee's brothers. He was Lord Fauconberg in right of his wife, the wealthy heiress Joan de Fauconberg or Falconbridge.

BLACK FULK OF ANJOU, 3RD COUNT OF ANJOU "FOULQUES NERRA" (born circa 965, died 1040). He married his cousin Elisabeth de Vendome, whom he accused of adultery. She was burned alive in the market place of Angers in 1000. By his second wife, Hildegard, he became the father of Geoffrey Martel. He is the ancestor of all of the Counts of Anjou, and via Henry II of England, of Cecylee and many of her friends. He earned the title "Black" because of his foul temper.

LADY ELEANOR TALBOT (born circa 1435), youngest daughter of John Talbot, 1st Earl of Shrewsbury and Margaret Beauchamp, Cecylee's dearest friend.

ANNE DE CAUX "ANNETTE" (dates unknown), nursemaid and governess to Cecylee's children.

PHILIPPE DE SAVOY, COUNT OF GENEVA (1417-1444). Youngest son of Count Amadeus VII of Savoy, who became the Antipope Felix V. Little is known about Philippe de Savoy, except that he never married.

Fictional characters:
PÈRE ANDRÉ, chaplain at Rouen Castle
AUDREY, Countess Joan's maid
CLAVIS, Cecylee's Irish Wolfhound
DOUCETTE, Cecylee's pony
MASTER ELBEUF, Richard's comptroller
DR. EUSEBIUS, Edward's tutor
GUNILDA, Anne's maid
JENET, Cecylee's' maid
JENKIN, Earl Ralph's page
PERREQUIN (PERKIN), Audrey's illegitimate son who made the
    sugar sculptures for Cecylee's betrothal.
PIERRE DE BLAY "BLAYBOURNE", Cecylee's lover
THOMASINA, Cath's maid

CPSIA information can be obtained at www.ICGtesting.com
Printed in the USA
BVOW011150010312

284206BV00010B/138/P